HEART'S RUN

Praise for D. Jackson Leigh

Unbridled

"A hot, steamy, erotic romance mystery with edge, exciting twists and turns, great characters and an unforgettable story that I was completely invested in. It was difficult to put the book down and I thoroughly enjoyed the whole experience of reading it!"
—*LESBIReviewed*

Blades of Bluegrass

"Both lead characters, Britt and Teddy, were well developed and likeable. I also really enjoyed the supporting characters, like E.B., and the warm, familiar atmosphere the author managed to create at Story Hill Farm."—*Melina Bickard, Librarian, Waterloo Library (UK)*

"*Blades of Bluegrass* was my first try of Leigh's books, and it sure won't be my last. If you love horses, military politics, or simply enjoy some wooing content, this book is for you."—*Hsinju's Lit Log*

Ordinary Is Perfect

"There's something incredibly charming about this small town romance, which features a vet with PTSD and a workaholic marketing guru as a fish out of water in the quiet town. But it's the details of this novel that make it shine."—*Pink Heart Society*

"D. Jackson Leigh knows how to write great romance, so I wasn't surprised that I enjoyed this one. It's easy to get into and it has a lovely happily ever after…Do you like age gap pairings, opposites attract, small town settings, butch/femme couples, and found family? If so, you'll want to pick up *Ordinary Is Perfect*. It's a sweet story and I especially recommend getting it in audio."—*Lesbian Review*

Take a Chance

"I really enjoyed the character dynamic with this book of two very strong independent women who aren't looking for love but fall for the one they already love…The chemistry and dynamic between these two is fantastic and becomes even more intense when their sexual desires take over."—*Les Rêveur*

Dragon Horse War

"Leigh writes with an emotion that she in turn gives to the characters, allowing us insight into their personalities and their very souls. Filled with fantastic imagery and the down-to-earth flaws that are sometimes the characters' greatest strengths, this first *Dragon Horse War* is a story not to be missed. The writing is flawless, the story, breath-taking—and this is only the beginning."—*Lambda Literary Review*

"The premise is original, the fantasy element is gripping but relevant to our times, the characters come to life, and the writing is phenomenal. It's the author's best work to date and I could not put it down."—*Melina Bickard, Librarian, Waterloo Library (UK)*

"Already an accomplished author of many romances, Leigh takes on fantasy and comes up aces…So, even if fantasy isn't quite your thing, you should give this a try. Leigh's backdrop is a world you already recognize with some slight differences, and the characters are marvelous. There's a villain, a love story, and…ah yes, 'thar be dragons.'"—*Out in Print: Queer Book Reviews*

"This book is great for those that like romance with a hint of fantasy and adventure."—*The Lesbrary*

"Skin Walkers" in *Women of the Dark Streets*

"When love persists through many lifetimes, there is always the potential magic of reunion. Climactically resplendent!"—*Rainbow Book Reviews*

Swelter

"I don't think there is a single book D. Jackson Leigh has written that I don't like…I recommend this book if you want a nice romance mixed with a little suspense."—*Kris Johnson, Texas Library Association*

"This book is a great mix of romance, action, angst, and emotional drama…The first half of the book focuses on the budding relationship between the two women, and the gradual revealing of secrets. The second half ramps up the action side of things…There were some good sexy scenes, and also an appropriate amount of angst and introspection by both women as feelings more than just the physical started to surface."—*Rainbow Book Reviews*

Call Me Softly

"*Call Me Softly* is a thrilling and enthralling novel of love, lies, intrigue, and Southern charm."—*Bibliophilic Book Blog*

Touch Me Gently

"D. Jackson Leigh understands the value of branding, and delivers more of the familiar and welcome story elements that set her novels apart from other authors in the romance genre."—*Rainbow Reader*

Every Second Counts

"Her prose is clean, lean, and mean—elegantly descriptive."—*Out in Print: Queer Book Reviews*

Riding Passion

"The sex was always hot and the relationships were realistic, each with their difficulties. The technical writing style was impeccable, ranging from poetic to more straightforward and simple. The entire anthology was a demonstration of Leigh's considerable abilities."—*2015 Rainbow Award*

By the Author

Romance

Call Me Softly

Touch Me Gently

Hold Me Forever

Swelter

Take a Chance

Ordinary Is Perfect

Blades of Bluegrass

Unbridled

Forever Comes in Threes

Here for You

When Tomorrow Comes

Unwrapped

Heart's Run

Cherokee Falls Series

Bareback

Long Shot

Every Second Counts

Dragon Horse War Trilogy

The Calling

Tracker and the Spy

Seer and the Shield

Short story collection

Riding Passion

Visit us at www.boldstrokesbooks.com

HEART'S RUN

by

D. Jackson Leigh

2025

HEART'S RUN

ISBN 13: 978-1-63679-825-7

This Trade Paperback Original Is Published By
Bold Strokes Books, Inc.
P.O. Box 249
Valley Falls, NY 12185

First Edition: November 2025

CREDITS

Editor: Shelley Thrasher
Production Design: Stacia Seaman
Cover Design by Tammy Seidick

Acknowledgments

Wow. This marks twenty books for me now. As always, I owe so much to my editor, Dr. Shelley Thrasher, who always makes my stories better. I value her friendship as well as her expertise. Also, I'm so grateful to the ever-supportive and brilliant Bold Strokes staff.

This one's for reader Carol from Colorado
who over the years has emailed me many times to ask
that I write a book about the wild horses.

I had a wonderful time learning about the wild horse herds
as I researched material for this story.

Chapter One

Tobie Mason led the Thoroughbred mare out of the bright sunlight into the cool interior of the slant-load trailer and swung the padded partition into place to secure her in the third stall. Another mare and a yearling colt were in the first two of the five-stall, fifth-wheel transport. "Is that it?"

"Yep." The manager of the Kentucky horse farm handed her a clipboard so she could sign the papers acknowledging she was properly insured and responsible for the horses until they were safely delivered to their California destination. "I know you said your transport could accommodate five, but the buyer decided to pay for all five stalls so his horses weren't exposed to others from another farm. Just a health safety precaution, you know."

After a quick read of the contract, Tobie scribbled her signature, then gave the clipboard back to the man. "It makes no difference to me. Less work for the price of a full trailer."

The man tore off a carbon copy of the agreement she signed and added it into an expanding file folder he returned to her. "This has all their health, breeding, and ownership transfer documents."

"Thanks."

He eyed the shiny white and silver goose-neck she was hauling with a Ford 350 dually truck. "Your rig looks brand new."

"It is." Tobie grinned at him. "They're the first to ride in it. I can't transport high-dollar horses in livestock trailers."

"It must have cost you a pretty penny. What'd you do? Rob a bank?"

She laughed and shook her head. "Sold the house my grandmother left me and special-ordered this to cut down the living quarters and add two more stalls." She patted the side of the trailer. "My life is on the road, so this is home now until I haul enough horses to put down roots again somewhere."

"Mind if I have a look inside?"

Tobie was proud to show off her acquisition. "It's aluminum with steel reinforcements to keep it light, and it has rear and side ramps for loading. There's storage for tack and feed behind the camper section." She opened the door to the large, roomy space in the front. "The bed is in the loft over the hitch, of course. This model usually sells with an area that has a sofa that makes into a second bed and a table that seats four across from the sofa. I cut that down in my redesign, so I only have a small kitchen with no dishwasher, and a two-burner stove and microwave. Next to it is a reclining chair with a board that folds down across it to be used for a table or desk. And across from that is all storage for food, clothes, and such, with a 22-inch TV attached to the cabinet door. The trailer has built-in 5G Wi-Fi, heating, and air conditioning."

"Perfect for one person, but it'd be a tight fit for two," the man said.

"I'm not planning on sharing the space. This is strictly for business."

"So, I'm guessing you aren't going to drive straight through to the West Coast."

"No. It's more than two thousand miles, thirty-one hours from Kentucky. That'd be too hard on the horses. I'll be stopping twice at farms where I've reserved a quarantine corral and barn space. I'll overnight there to give them a break from standing in these snug stalls. So, the buyer can expect me in about three days. I have his phone number if any unanticipated delays come up."

"That's good to know." He shook his head. "I can't believe the boss is selling that last mare you loaded."

"I was under the impression he was selling all his horses and getting out of the racing business."

"He is, but I thought he might at least keep her."

"Why's that?"

He looked over at the adjacent pasture, his brow knitting and his mouth turning down. "Sarah's Heart belonged to his daughter.

She raised Heart herself from a foal, then trained her for the track. She did really well, too. Won or placed in all her races. After Sarah died, I guess he just couldn't stand to look at the horse. Miss Sarah was special to all of us, and she sure loved that horse." He seemed to shake himself from the memory and turned back to her. "She's a five-year-old that hasn't raced in a year, so he sold her as breeding stock. At least she's going to a good farm."

Tobie offered her hand, and he shook it. "I promise to take good care of her."

He nodded. "You do that. I like to think she'll be running around a big pasture with a baby at her side one day."

❖

The sky had turned dark and threatening, and Tobie could see the downpour literally moving across the plain toward her. Still, she grinned at the road sign. "Looks like we're two-thirds of the way there. We won't be stopping anymore except for gas and grub," she said to nobody.

Life on the road could get lonely for some people, but Tobie liked her own company. She often thought about getting a dog to travel with her, but she'd been so busy running short hauls and selling her grandmother's property to raise the money for this long-haul rig she hadn't had time to devote much thought to what kind of dog she'd want. Maybe she'd spend some time thinking about that subject and check out some shelters once she made this delivery.

After the past year of nonstop hauling jobs, she had the next month open. She planned to find a nice campsite in the mountains where she could do some fly-fishing or maybe something on a gulf-side beach where she could watch the ocean waves.

She drove into the curtain of rain and switched on her wipers, glad she'd left the sharp highway curves of the Colorado Rockies behind her an hour ago. Then it really began to rain. Visibility was so poor, she could barely see the taillights of the eighteen-wheeler in front of her. She slowed to put some distance between her and the rig ahead, just to be safe, but when she realized she was white-knuckling the steering wheel, she decided to leave the interstate highway at the next exit and wait until the storm let up or passed entirely. Her new truck and trailer were worth a quarter million dollars, not to mention that the three racing Thoroughbreds she was hauling were worth insured for more than a million dollars together.

Tobie let out a relieved breath when she passed a road sign indicating an exit in two miles. Hopefully there would be a truck stop, or at least a gas station, where she could sit out this deluge. The thought had barely cleared her brain when a jacked-up pickup truck raced past her. Shaking her head at the driver's foolishness, she stiffened as the truck hydroplaned in front of her, skidded sideways, and disappeared into the rain ahead. She slowed more, glancing in her mirrors nervously in case some unprepared motorist behind her didn't notice her brake lights soon enough to keep from rear-ending her trailer.

When she looked ahead again, she faced a huge mass of careening metal and tires blocking both lanes in her path. In that split second she had checked her mirrors, the pickup had apparently slid into the eighteen-wheeler, causing it to jackknife out of control.

She hit her brakes so hard, she could smell the rubber burning. But the roadway was wet and slick, even under her brand-new tires. She prayed she could stop before the eighteen-wheeler quit sliding down the road, but she continued to skid forward. At the last minute, the pickup careened off the roadway and into the field on the left, leaving an opening for her to go onto the roadway's shoulder and around the big tractor-trailer. When she came to a stop, her heart was pounding in her ears. She'd missed any collision, but the road shoulder was too soft for the weight of her loaded trailer, and the wheels dug into the mud before she could get back on the pavement.

Her legs wobbled from the adrenaline rush when she stepped out of her truck and pulled on her waterproof duster, so she paused a moment while the rain pelted her and streamed off the brim of her ball cap. She needed to check on the horses. They were likely already on edge from the noise of the initial crash and the following collisions as two other vehicles failed to stop and smashed into the jack-knifed eighteen-wheeler.

When Tobie rounded the big rig to reach the back of her trailer, she almost smacked into a large, bearded man.

"You okay?" he asked.

"Yeah, but my trailer is stuck in the mud. You okay?"

The trucker spit a wad of chewing tobacco onto the road. "Damn near swallowed my chaw, but I'm not hurt. I'd like to smack that stupid boy in the pickup that caused all this."

"You and me both. What idiot doesn't know to slow down when it's raining this hard?" She peered through the rain at the skinny twenty-something who was swearing over his damaged truck even though blood was pouring from his forehead. "Anybody in those cars hurt?"

"Nothing major in the SUV, but I'm afraid to look at the car that's shoved under my trailer. It's going to take some major equipment to pry it open. I've already radioed the highway patrol. They said they're about twenty minutes out, but the local sheriff and the fire department should be here in a few minutes."

"I need to check on my horses. I'll wait for them in my trailer." At his nod, she went to the trailer and lowered the rear ramp. The shoulder's slope was slight, but the tires on the off-side had sunk deeply into the mud when the weight of the three horses, each about a thousand pounds, had shifted toward the tilt. Damn. She'll have to unload the horses before trying to pull the trailer free, but she'd wait for help.

The mare closest to her, Heart, nickered when she opened the trailer, but the gray yearling's eyes were wide with fright as he shifted in his confined space, kicking several times against the side of the trailer. This was a dangerous situation. If he didn't calm down, he could hurt himself or the horses on either side of him.

She opened the metal first-aid box embedded in the side of the trailer and found the mild sedative she always carried. After drawing out a good dose of the medicine into a syringe, she approached the horses. She stroked Heart for a minute before ducking under her neck to reach the yearling. She talked softly while she felt along his neck for the artery she needed, then waited until he settled a few seconds before quickly popping the needle into his skin. He drummed his feet again, but she'd already injected the sedative and withdrawn the needle before his second hoof hit the rubber mat covering the floor. His kicking wound down to a few indignant snorts within minutes, his eyes softening. He let out a long breath that sounded like a sigh of relief and reached down to snuffle some hay that had dropped from his feed bag.

The mare in the front stall was munching her hay and seemed unaffected by their harrowing near collision, so Tobie sat down next to Heart's stall and stared out at the downpour while she waited for assistance.

❖

The storm intensified. Lightning lit up the sky, and booming thunder seemed to grow closer as the minutes ticked by. The gray colt's head hung low in a sedated doze, but the mares began to fidget inside the confinement of their narrow stalls, rocking the trailer and causing it to tilt even more. Tobie was relieved when she spotted the emergency lights of the police and firemen.

She stepped back into the rain and approached the fire chief, who was talking to a pair of policemen. "Hey. I need some assistance pretty soon. I've got three very expensive horses in that trailer, and it's stuck in the mud. I had to drive onto the shoulder to miss that eighteen-wheeler. I need to unload the horses and get my trailer back on the road."

"Are any of your animals injured? Do you need a vet on the scene?"

"No, but I've already had to sedate one, and the other two are getting restless because of the thunder."

"Then we'll get to you, miss, but we need to get the people out of that car that's stuck under the rig first."

"I understand, but—"

"I can help you," the younger of the two deputies said. "I grew up around horses and still rodeo some."

Tobie was relieved. She really didn't want to sedate the mares. "Great. I really appreciate it."

They stepped into the trailer, and she clipped a rope lead onto Heart's halter before releasing her from the stall tether and swinging the near side of the stall open. The deputy waited at the bottom of the rear ramp for her to exit, and she handed Heart's lead rope to him. Squinting against the rain, she pointed to a small group of scrubby trees that grew in the meadow at the foothills of the Rockies. "Tie her over there, away from all this wreckage. I'll get the other two."

He nodded and led Heart away while she turned back to the

other horses. The mare was a little skittish, but the colt was quiet and easily led from the trailer. She had almost reached the trees when thunder boomed overhead. The colt only flinched, but the mare reared, eyes wide and nostrils flaring. Tobie quickly brought her under control, but when she turned around, Heart was dragging the deputy across the field.

He wasn't a big man, and his weight wasn't slowing the horse down much. He held on for about fifty yards as the frightened mare pulled him through prickly brush and rocks until his head and shoulder slammed into a saddle-sized boulder and he went limp.

"Officer down, officer down," Tobie shouted, hoping someone could hear her over the rain. She made sure the other two horses were tied securely, then ran to where the deputy was beginning to stir. He groaned and rolled over as she approached, but his eyes were unfocused. He was covered in mud and blood from scratches on his face and arms. She leaned over him to shelter his face from the rain. "Hey. You okay?"

He blinked at her but didn't answer before an EMT brushed her aside. "We've got this," the woman said as her partner carrying a medical box joined her.

Tobie stood and stared after Heart, a ghostly figure in the storm, racing toward the foothills.

Chapter Two

Maggie Wilkes emptied a scoop of kibble into the bowl of her border collie, Kate, then poured herself a cup of coffee and added a liberal amount of creamer and sugar. Her sister often teased her, saying it wasn't coffee by the time Maggie finished fixing it up. Call it latte if you want, she always told her sister, but she liked it that way.

She settled into a chair at the kitchen table that doubled as her workspace but didn't open her laptop. Instead, she gazed out at the thunderous rain through the window in the top half of her back door. She didn't mind that the storm was ferocious because the grassy plains where her wild horses grazed were desperate for nourishment. She didn't worry about the horses. The herds had survived hundreds of years through many storms, blizzards, and droughts. They would have sensed the storm coming and taken shelter in the area's heavily forested valleys.

She did worry, though, about the possibility of tornadoes, so she opened her laptop and checked a local television station's website for any warnings. Their Doppler radar didn't show any twisters, but a report on a serious pileup on the highway just outside of town caught her eye. Their reporter was broadcasting live from the scene.

"We don't have the name of the driver yet, but witnesses said the accident was caused by that pickup truck." The reporter was struggling to point at the vehicle while holding a microphone in one hand and an umbrella in the other. "Firefighters are working to free the occupants pinned in a car wedged under a jackknifed tractor-trailer." Maggie was about to scroll back to the weather report when the camera panned the scene and a large horse trailer came into view. She jumped up from her chair and went to the kitchen counter, where she kept a police scanner. Flipping it on, she tuned into the channel where she knew local police and firefighters talked to each other.

"We've got an officer down."

Loud static sounded when she turned up the volume, and then several clicks were followed by the voice of the fire-department captain in charge of the scene. "How bad?"

"Hit his head on a rock and was out for a minute, but he's awake and talking now."

"Hit his head on a rock?"

"Horse dragged him through some cactus and underbrush, and he finally let go when his head connected with the rock. He's scratched up pretty good, and bloody, and the medics say he needs a few stitches in his head, but he'll be okay."

"Get one of the deputies to drive him to the hospital. We're close to getting this woman out that's trapped in the car, and we're going to need the ambulance for her."

"Ten-four...Captain?"

"Go ahead."

"The horse took off, and the driver of that rig is having a fit about it. Says that it's a high-dollar animal."

"We don't have time to worry about a horse right now. Anyway, there's no way we'd be able to find it in this storm. Just see what you can do about getting her trailer out of the mud."

"We unhitched the truck from the trailer, but Joe says he can't hook up to the trailer because it's a fifth-wheel. Maybe we can get the truck driver to disconnect from his trailer after you remove the car under it and hook up to the horse trailer to pull it back on the road."

"It'll be a while," the captain said. "We're likely going to have to cut that car into pieces to get it free."

"Ten-four," the deputy replied.

"Idiots," Maggie said, even though only Kate was listening. "Just because it's a fifth-wheel doesn't mean its gooseneck is compatible with an eighteen-wheeler's hitch." She checked the location of the accident in the maps app on her phone. It wasn't more than two miles away. She pulled on her waterproof, full-length duster and tall muck boots. The rain had frizzed her curly brown hair, so she wove it into a quick braid and donned her leather Outback hat. She'd been caught in quick summer rainstorms many times while shadowing one of the wild horse herds, so she knew how to dress for the worst weather.

"Come on, Kate. Let's go rescue that horse person from our clueless law enforcement." She strode through the puddles of her muddy driveway to the tall metal building that was her equipment shed and her semi-truck she used for pulling two large gooseneck trailers needed when she harvested the sorghum she grew to financially sustain the farm she'd inherited from her father. Boosting Kate and then herself into the truck's high cab, she settled her phone into its holder and punched in the sheriff's cell phone number.

Sheriff Dan Chandler answered after the second ring. "Kind of busy, Maggie."

"I know. Been listening to the scanner. I'm just calling to let you know I'm on my way in my semi. It can hook up to a gooseneck and pull that horse trailer out of the mud for you."

"That would be great. I should have thought of you before now. We've got a huge mess that's going to take hours to clear. We can use all the help we can get. What's your ETA?"

"I'm only about two miles out. See you in five." She ended the call.

Maggie was glad to see that she was on the front side of the pileup, so pulling the horse trailer back onto the road would be easy. She swung around in the roadway and backed up to the front of the trailer before hopping out. "Stay in the truck, Kate. Too many vehicles are coming and going for you to be running around." Kate whined but settled back to keep vigil from the driver's seat.

Maggie whistled when Sheriff Chandler walked over to meet her. "That's some fancy rig. Looks brand new." She studied the wheels mired deep in the dark mud of the road's shoulder. "It's stuck in there pretty good."

"It's got to be nearly forty feet long. Think you can pull it out?"

"Might be big, but that's an aluminum body, so it's not all that heavy. Where's the owner? I need to get permission to hook up in case something gets bent or broken while I'm dragging it out of the mud."

"On the other side, in that stand of trees with two of the horses." He pointed in the general direction indicated. "Thought it was best to unload them in case things go sideways when we try to pull it free." Rain sluiced off the front of his Resistol Western hat when he turned and ducked his head to spit a stream of tobacco juice. Maggie found chewing tobacco even more disgusting than smoking.

She nodded and rounded the horse trailer. She could barely see the shadowy figures of two horses through the sheets of rain, but three human figures materialized in the gloom as she strode toward them. She recognized her nephew, who was a deputy sheriff, arguing with one of the firefighter medics. The third person had their back to Maggie, but they wore a duster identical to her own and a ball cap pulled low over shaggy blond hair darkened by rainwater.

"I'm looking for the owner of that horse trailer." She was surprised when a woman turned to her. Not many females bested her own five-foot-eight height, but this woman had at least four inches on her. Brown eyes studied her while a long, silent second passed between them before the woman stuck her hand out.

"Tobie Mason. I'm the owner."

Maggie cleared her throat. "I need your permission to hook up to your trailer and pull it out of the mud."

Tobie glanced toward the mired transport. "My three-fifty dually couldn't pull it out, so I doubt a tow truck will do it."

"I heard over the police scanner that a gooseneck was stuck in the mud, so I drove my semi over to help. It's outfitted to hitch to a standard gooseneck."

Tobie nodded. "If that won't do it, I don't know what will."

Maggie started to turn back to the wreckage, then stopped when she saw her nephew's battered face and the bloody cloth he held to the side of his head. "What in the world, Ricky? Were you in that pileup?"

Ricky shook his head, then winced at the movement. "No. I was walking this lady's third horse to these trees when a big crack of thunder spooked it. The damned horse dragged me through a pile of cactus."

"He only let go when his head hit a rock and it knocked him out," the medic said. "Maybe you can persuade this idiot to go to the hospital to get checked out."

"I'm fine," Ricky said. "I've had worse falls riding bulls at the rodeo."

Maggie frowned at him. "I'm not going to stand out here in the rain and argue with you, boy. Stay with these horses while we get that trailer out of the mud, and then go to the hospital."

"I don't need a doctor."

She pointed a finger at him. "I'll call your mama and tell her you have a brain injury."

"God damn it. She'll panic and show up here crying and carrying on."

"At the very least." She pulled her cell phone from her pocket as though she was about to call.

"Okay, okay. I'll go."

The medic grinned. "Wish I'd thought of that," he said.

Maggie shot her nephew one last stern look, then headed back to the trailer in long strides.

Tobie checked again that her horses were tied securely and took a long look in the direction in which Heart had disappeared into the downpour, then followed the woman with laser-blue eyes, who she hoped would solve at least the first of her problems.

Several of the firemen shoveled mud from around the trailer's double tires, while Tobie watched the semi maneuver expertly into position to couple with her gooseneck. She flipped open the control panel and pressed the buttons that retracted the front stabilizers to slowly lower the ball of her gooseneck so it locked in the jaw of the semi's hitch when it backed up the final inches. Perfect.

After she signaled for the semi to pull forward, she yelled for the firemen to get their shovels clear. The semi's engine revved, then pulled forward slow and steady until the trailer was free and back on the highway pavement.

"Yes!" Tobie pumped the air with her fist and rushed forward to unhook from the semi. When it pulled away, she stepped back and headed over to thank her rescuer, but the semi didn't stop. "Thank you," she yelled, and the woman merely waved in acknowledgment.

Whatever. Tobie had business to tend to.

Ricky helped her load the mare and yearling colt into the trailer again. "I need to find my other horse," she said, tying off the yearling's lead rope. "And you need to see a doctor."

"I'm going. If I don't, my aunt will call my mother. She tends toward hysterics, and dealing with her would just make my headache worse." His smile was more like a grimace. "But you ain't going to find your other horse in this storm. It's not due to blow out of here for another twelve hours. I know a lot of people don't believe it, but climate change is a real thing. We rarely had storms like this when I was a boy, but this one is the fourth this year. I know several folks that would rent you a few stalls for the night. Then you could look for your horse in the morning."

Tobie shook her head. "Can't do that. These aren't actually my horses. I'm just contracted to haul them to a Thoroughbred farm in California. I can't stable them just anywhere along the way because it would break their quarantine, and the buyer could refuse delivery."

Ricky glanced at her Kentucky license plate. "Are these racers?"

"Yep. The one that got away is going to be hell to catch. She won quite a few races and is being retired for breeding because she has Secretariat in her bloodline." She opened the mapping app on her phone and calculated her options. "I'm about twelve hours away, so I'll deliver these two and come back for the mare in about twenty-four hours. The weather should be better for searching then."

"I can spread the word around for folks to look out for her. She might show up at somebody's barn, looking for food and shelter." He touched the bloody bandage on his head. My brain's a little fuzzy. Remind me what she looks like."

"She's a dark bay with one white sock." She went to her cab and flipped through the paperwork on her clipboard. "Her lip tattoo is X74826."

Ricky wrote the number in a small pad he carried in his shirt pocket. "Got it."

Tobie shook the young man's hand. "Appreciate your help. And I'm sorry my horse dragged you halfway to the mountains. I think I can still see some cactus needles sticking out of your cheek."

He laughed but winced when he touched his face. "Yeah. Better get those out before Mama sees me." He handed her a card with his badge and phone numbers on it. "Give me a call when you get back, and I'll let you know if we've had any sightings of your missing mare."

She took the card and smiled. She liked this guy. "I'll do that," she said.

Chapter Three

Maggie backed her semi into the equipment shed and ran through the rain toward the house. But she slid to a stop as she neared a huge oak split down the middle and still smoking. "Damned lightning. That tree's stood for more than a hundred years." She didn't know that for certain, but it was likely. She shed her duster, hat, and boots in the mudroom, and then, in her socked feet, padded into the kitchen, where she heard voices. But when she realized the voices were coming from the small television she'd apparently forgotten to turn off when she'd left earlier, she relaxed.

"Police have confirmed one fatality and at least five injured in this huge pileup on Highway 50 about five miles east of the state line. Several people involved in the accident say the driver of a red pickup was responsible for initiating the chain reaction of crashes." The camera panned to show a red truck with a "Make America Great Again" sticker and a beer logo plastered on the back window of the cab. "Sheriff Dan Chandler, however, said he won't name that driver until his investigation is complete, and only if charges are warranted."

Maggie snorted. "Hell. Everybody in town knows that truck belongs to the Bradley boy." Kate gave a sharp yip in agreement.

"The sheriff is asking that everyone in the surrounding community be on the lookout for a horse that escaped from a trailer involved in the pileup." The camera had panned back to the newswoman. "We're told it's a bay—that's brown for non-horse people—mare, with one white sock. We're also told it's a Thoroughbred racing horse accustomed to being stabled, so it might seek shelter and food at someone's barn. Anyone who sees this horse should call the sheriff's department immediately."

"If that horse has any sense, it'll stay out there where it's free," Maggie said. "You know they keep those racehorses stalled up to twenty-three hours of the day to get them hopped up to race. And they run them while they're still babies, before their bones are fully grown. That's why so many break legs on the track."

Curled up in her bed, Kate seemed to have lost interest in this lesson on Thoroughbred racing. She gave only a weak wag of her tail and closed her eyes.

Maggie had forgotten to turn off the coffeepot, so it was still warm even though the coffee was probably a bit overbrewed. That didn't really matter, though, after she diluted it with milk and sweetened it with several tablespoons of sugar.

After settling down with her coffee au lait, she opened her laptop connected to two large-screen monitors to check her trail cameras. She had nine in all, three posted at water holes frequented by the wild horses in her area and the rest stationed along various trails and meadows where they traveled and grazed. She ignored the watering holes, since none would be drinking during this deluge, and opened the camera feeds on the trails that wound through the foothills and valley forests.

The storm made for poor visibility, but she caught sight of movement off to the side of one trail. Yes! Horses were moving restlessly among the tall pines and spruces that provided a bit of protection from the driving rain. She couldn't tell which group was sheltering there, but it appeared to be one of the larger families.

Cattle ranchers who wanted all federal grazing grounds reserved for their herds liked to convince the public that the wild horses amassed in huge groups that would sweep through like locusts and denude a well-grassed field in hours. The horses normally grouped in small families of five to maybe fifteen at the most. While stallions would defend their mares from young studs trying to start their own family, they didn't constantly try to steal mares from other established groups. It wasn't uncommon for two groups to peacefully visit a pond at the same time.

Stallions usually decided if a young challenger in their group should be expelled. But each family had a dominant female that served as the boss mare. She decided if a new filly or a young, non-dominant male was allowed to join or stay in their group.

Maggie was about to close the camera app when movement in a corner frame caught her eye. This camera was stationed at a higher meadow in the foothills, which was one of the Cloud herd's favorite grazing spots. The storm apparently had dislodged her trail camera so that it was pointing toward a low overhang in a rocky cliff face on the backside of the field. She knew it well because she often camped there when gathering data on the wild horses.

"There you are." She squinted at the dark form huddled under the overhang with its backside to the driving rain. Visibility was too poor to tell for sure, but this was a single horse. Any wild horses would be huddled with their herd for added shelter against the weather.

She sipped her coffee and watched the lone horse. Should she let Sheriff Chandler know she'd spotted the missing mare? There was a lot to consider. This horse knew nothing about survival in the wild, and it'd grown up on a precise diet of quality feed and hay. It might not survive on the coarse grass of the plains. Also, the mare might prefer the company of humans since it had been handled from birth. It was likely drawn to the rock shelter by the lingering human scent of her recent camp there. On the other hand, would recapture doom it to a life of confinement and forced breeding if her racing career was over?

Ultimately, it wasn't her horse or her decision. Maggie closed her laptop and walked to the sink to toss out the last of her coffee. It was growing late, and the steady pelt of rain on her metal roof was making her drowsy. She would let fate determine that mare's future. She had sorghum and corn fields to harvest once this rain quit and the fields dried out. Fall was fast approaching. Someone else could chase the wayward horse.

Chapter Four

Tobie yawned as she turned into the driveway of the Thoroughbred farm located about a hundred miles northeast of the Santa Anita Park racetrack. It had been a grueling twelve-hour drive with a few brief stops to refill her cooler with Red Bull and grab a truck-stop sandwich when she had to fill her truck with more diesel.

It'd been a long haul for the horses, too, so she was anxious to unload and walk them around. She parked in front of a series of single-story barns typical of racing stables. If they had a second story, it was normally outfitted to house grooms and other workers. Hay was kept in a separate, metal building to negate the risk of fire.

She pulled her ball cap low over her sunglasses. She desperately needed a shower and real food because all the caffeine she'd consumed was burning a hole in her stomach, so she was glad to see several men immediately approach from the nearest barn. She hopped down from the truck and grabbed her clipboard.

"Are you Miss Mason?" the first man to reach her asked.

"That's me."

"I'm the farm manager."

She shook his offered hand. "Sorry I'm a half day late. Ran into some really bad weather and a big pileup this side of the Rockies. I've been driving for the last twelve hours, so I'd like to get the horses out and exercising before we deal with the paperwork."

He called over the two men who'd followed him from the barn. "Let's unload these horses and walk them around a bit before we put them in the quarantine barn."

They all went to the back of Tobie's rig, and the men waited while she unloaded and handed off the yearling and the remaining mare.

The farm manager scratched his head. "I was expecting another mare."

Tobie handed over her clipboard. "There were three. A tractor-trailer rig jackknifed in front of me during a bad storm, causing a multi-car pileup. I managed to steer around them, but my trailer got stuck in the mud on the road's shoulder. I had to unload the horses so we could pull it back on the road, and one mare spooked when lightning struck nearby and took off for the hills after she dragged a deputy through a pile of cactus and rocks. Sarah's Heart was the one that escaped."

He looked up sharply from the paperwork he was studying. "That's damned bad luck. She's the most high-dollar one among the three."

"I drove straight through the night to unload these two so I can go back and find her."

He frowned, his friendly demeanor disappearing. "If you can even find her, how are you going to catch a racehorse on those plains? I don't want her chased down with a helicopter and injured."

Tobie shook her head. "I was thinking a bucket of grain might do the trick if I can get close. I figure she's missing her morning feed by now."

"And what if you don't find her or you do come across only her carcass because a bear or wolves got her?"

He had a right to be angry about the horse, but Tobie was tired, and he was wearing on her last nerve. "Well, they'd have to catch her to eat her. But if something did make a meal of her, or she's broken a leg running through those mountains, I'm fully insured. Your boss will get his money back even if I can't deliver your horse." She pointed to her clipboard he held. "I just need your signature that you've received the other two, and I'll be heading back."

She watched him scribble his signature with a note that Sarah's Heart remained missing.

"I'll give you two weeks to locate my horse, and then I'm filing a claim with your insurance company," he said, handing the papers back to her.

She tore off the carbon copy underneath and gave it to him.

"Normally, I'd hang around to give you time for a vet check of those two, but you can contact me if you find any problems. I need to get back and look for your other horse."

Tobie had intended to ask if she could park her rig on the farm to get a quick shower and grab a few hours of sleep, but she climbed back into her truck instead. She wasn't feeling very welcome here. She'd park at the truck stop and diner she'd seen about thirty miles back.

❖

Tobie slid her sunglasses in place as she opened the door to her trailer's living quarters and stepped out into the late-afternoon sun. The truck stop had been a good choice, with clean showers, plenty of hot water, and a diner that served some of the best roast and gravy she'd tasted west of the Mississippi. It even had a dump station where she could empty her sewage tank. Now, after four hours of deep sleep, she felt refreshed and ready to roll.

The return trip to the accident scene wouldn't take as long since she wasn't hauling live cargo. She could drive faster and with less caution around curves. As she watched the lines of the pavement zip by, she dialed the number the sheriff's deputy had given her.

"Hey, is this Ricky?"

"Yeah. Who's this?"

"Tobie Mason. The hauler that lost a horse in your county."

His attitude instantly changed from suspicious to friendly. "Oh, hey. Did you drop off your other horses?"

"Early this morning. I'm headed back now. I expect to get there tomorrow morning. Is there a campground nearby where I can leave my trailer until I locate my mare?"

"The only campground might have already closed for the season, but I can ask around. We have plenty of farms where you can park your rig. The only good hotels are a half hour away, but we do have an okay motel."

"I don't need housing. My trailer has living quarters. That's why I was asking about a campground."

"Oh. Good to know if I'm going to find you a place for it. Give me a call when you're close, and I'll tell you what I've found out."

❖

A tall man with piercing blue eyes was opening the gate when Tobie arrived at Fairview Campgrounds. She lowered her window as she pulled up beside him. "Hey. Thanks for accommodating me. Ricky said you guys had already closed to visitors."

The man nodded and smiled. "You must be Tobie." He held out his hand. "I'm Brice, and this is my campground. How about I ride along to show you where to park?"

"Hop in."

His tanned, leathery face and white hair didn't match his smooth gait and athletic launch into her passenger seat. "How long you planning to stay?" he asked. "I've closed my bookings so I can do some maintenance on the roads and campsites. Then, in two weeks, I'm shutting down for the winter and heading to Florida to fish with my brother." They drove past a log cabin that appeared to be the campsite office and his residence.

"I hope to catch my wayward horse and be gone by then."

He laughed. "Yeah. Ricky briefed me on that. Good luck running down a racehorse if she's on the open plains."

She laughed with him. "She's used to pampering—a bucket of grain twice a day and plenty of high-quality hay. I'm hoping that if I can get near her, I can lure her with some grain."

"That might work, but how are you going to track her down?"

Tobie shrugged. "Not sure. Unfortunately, nobody has reported seeing her around any of the nearby farms. I guess I'll go back to where she took off and see if I can find her still in that area, or at least see tracks that'll tell me which direction she's headed."

"Several wild horse herds are in that area. Probably hoof prints everywhere."

"Yes, but my horse is wearing shoes."

"Good point." He pointed to the left. "You can take that site. It has a pull-through and is near the river. Do you fish?"

"I fly-fish a little, but transporting horses keeps me busy and on the road. I don't expect to have any time for that here."

"Too bad. Folks come here for trout. I'm already booked up for next spring, when they're most plentiful. Fly-fishing is a great way to relax."

"That sounds good, and I wish I had time, but the mare's owner is only giving me two weeks to find her. Then he plans to file a claim with my insurance company. That'll blow my rates out of the water, so I'll be heading back to his farm as soon as I catch her."

"Since you're in a hurry, you should go see Wild Maggie. If a horse is wandering around, she'd know where to find it."

"And where do I find Wild Maggie?"

"Take a left onto the highway. In the middle of town, look for Cindy's Diner. If Maggie's not there eating dinner, Cindy can tell you how to get to her farm."

"I'll do that. I need to go into town for a few groceries anyway."

"Do you need any help getting set up?"

"Nope. It's fully electronic."

He nodded. "That's a fancy rig for sure. Well, I'll walk back and leave you to settle in. If you need anything, you can find me either at the cabin or somewhere along the river, fishing."

"Thanks, Brice. I appreciate you letting me stay even though you're closed for campers."

Chapter Five

The sun finally broke through when the winds following the storm pushed the dense clouds toward the mountains. Maggie stared at the distant peaks. The days were still warm, but she could already see some snow at the higher elevations.

She planted only about two hundred of her thousand acres in sorghum. Much of her land was too rocky to cultivate and the forest too beautiful to clear. She always harvested the sorghum early to provide income for the farm but took only one cutting of the hardy hay she planted in her far pastures. The sorghum grain was becoming a more popular crop because it could be milled for flour, or even syrup, and the stalks stored as silage for cows. But sorghum could be poison for horses, so she plowed the harvested fields under for the winter. The hay she baled mid-summer would feed her dairy goats and her riding mule over the winter. Rather than take a second cutting, she would open her hay fields to the wild horses to graze during the barren winter months.

She sold her goats' milk and cheese at the farmers' market and on the internet. The farm income, combined with the money she made from donations to her wild horses website, supported her comfortable, though not lavish, lifestyle.

Having fed her chickens and goats for the morning, she saddled her mule, Penny, filled a flour sack with grain, and headed out to where she'd seen the wayward mare on the trail camera, Kate following close behind.

She'd barely ridden a mile when her cell phone vibrated in her pocket. She almost ignored it, but it could be one of her elderly or disabled friends who needed her help from time to time. "What's up?" She never answered with a simple "hello."

"I was wondering if you'd spotted that missing horse on any of your trail cameras," Ricky said.

"What if I did?"

"That hauler is back in town to search for it. I thought if you'd seen it, I could give her an idea where to begin."

Maggie sighed, quickly thinking over her response. "Are you kidding? Every living thing was denned up or hiding in the forest to escape the storm if they had any sense." She didn't want to lie to her nephew, but she could talk around it.

"Are you at home? Sounds like you're riding."

"Penny, Kate, and I are out checking fences to see if any trees blew down on them. Lightning took out the big oak in my front yard."

"Dang. That's a shame. It was more than a hundred years old, wasn't it?"

"I reckon." She loved Ricky, but he was easy to distract from any subject she didn't want to discuss. "Look. I've got some goat cheese for your mother. Tell her I'll bring it by in a day or two."

"Okay. You take care out there, Aunt Maggie."

"Will do, kiddo. Talk to you later."

It wasn't long before she came across the tracks of a group of unshod horses. They appeared to be headed to the meadow where she'd spotted the mare. This could be a good thing or a bad thing, depending on the little herd's attitude toward adopting a new member. She reined in Penny as they approached the edge of the woods surrounding the field.

Cloud, the herd's stallion, was standing guard—ears twitching and nose raised to catch any sound or scent of a predator. The mares and a few juvenile colts grazed hungrily at the grass now succulent from the earlier rain, but she saw no sign of the missing mare, so she turned Penny away from the foothills and toward the flat, open plains.

She'd ridden for an hour before she burst from the trees onto a sea of waving grass. Pulling out her field binoculars, she spotted two families of wild horses grazing a safe distance from each other. She recognized the stallions as Indian and Night, both sired by Cloud. Several of the horses raised their heads in her direction but returned to grazing after a long stare. She was a familiar sight and long ago deemed non-threatening.

Maggie was about to turn toward home when she spotted a lone horse in the distance. It stood motionless. She raised her binoculars and confirmed that it fit the description of the escaped Thoroughbred, likely a full hand—four inches—taller than the mustangs. Lean, deep-chested, and long-legged, the horse was built for racing. The mare was staring at the other horses and scenting the air as if deciding whether to approach.

Night spotted the intruder and trotted toward her, head and tail raised high. When he had nearly reached her, the mare turned and ran. The stallion raced after her, but he was no match for her speed. He turned back to his herd, and the Thoroughbred disappeared into the distance.

Maggie shook her head. Even with her speed, the mare wouldn't survive in the wild unless she joined a herd for protection. Wolves were common in the area, and bears were frantically feeding in preparation for hibernation. She would try again tomorrow. Perhaps if she got close enough, the mare would follow her back to the farm. Then Maggie could maybe help her find a wild family. If that failed and the mare didn't appear to be thriving in a wild setting, only then would she turn her in to live out her life in service to men.

Ricky's patrol car was parked next to her house when Maggie returned, and he joined her in the barn as she unsaddled Penny.

"I don't suppose you saw that mare while you were out checking fences," he said.

She didn't look his way. "I saw several of the wild groups."

He was quiet for a long minute. "Would you tell me if you did see her?"

She plopped her saddle onto its rack and grabbed the tools to brush Penny down and check her feet for stones. "Why are you so interested in catching that woman's horse?"

"It's expensive, and I feel responsible for it getting loose. Besides, it's used to being pampered and probably won't survive in the wild."

"Maybe even a year of freedom is better than five penned up in a stall most of her life."

Ricky huffed. "I don't see you giving up your warm house and indoor plumbing to go live in the woods. And what about Penny? You keep her penned up and fed."

"I tried letting her loose, but she kept coming back to the farm. That mule would live in my house if I let her. In fact, she did come tromping into my kitchen one day when I'd propped the door open to bring in groceries. I believe she thinks she's a big dog."

Ricky pulled a stalk from the hay bales stored in the next stall and silently chewed on it. "Well, I'm hoping that racehorse will show up at someone's barn, looking for food and shelter."

Maggie put her brush and hoof pick away, then rewarded Penny with a scoop of sweet feed in her feed pan. The stall opened on the outside to the goat pasture, where she kept a large water trough filled. Unless the weather was bad, Penny would spend her time grazing among the goats and guarding them from predators. "Is that horse the only reason you came by here?" The mule stomped her foot when Kate darted forward to grab a mouthful of sweet feed for herself.

Ricky trailed along as she headed for the house. "I'm checking with most of the local farms, asking them to contact me if the horse turns up."

"Well, since you're here, come on inside and let me give you that goat cheese for your mother."

"She sure loves that stuff." He sat down at the kitchen table and opened her laptop. "Have you checked your trail cameras?"

Maggie took several logs of the soft cheese and wrapped them in white butcher paper, then plopped them on the table next to him. "Yes, I have." Standing next to him, she closed the laptop. "Now go on and mind your own business."

He pushed back from the table and stood. "Geez, you're grouchy."

"My back is sore from riding the fence all day."

"I don't know why you don't take the four-wheeler to check on fences."

"Because Penny likes to hit the trail with me and Kate once in a while."

He picked up the package of cheese and kissed her on the cheek before turning to leave. "Call me if you see that horse."

"Yeah, yeah, yeah," she said, knowing she wouldn't.

Chapter Six

Tobie zipped the fleece vest that matched her blue flannel shirt. The sun was barely up, and the morning held a brisk hint of autumn. She'd unhitched her truck from the trailer the day before when she set up her camp, but she'd been too tired to go anywhere after only four hours of sleep. So, she climbed into it now to head to town. The parking lot of Cindy's Diner in the center of the small downtown had been full when she drove through the day before, so she figured the food was good there.

Nothing chimed or rang when she stepped through the glass door, but every head in the restaurant turned her way. "Morning," she said to nobody and everybody, giving a little wave before taking a seat at the counter.

A middle-aged waitress with *Cindy* on her name tag immediately plopped a white ceramic coffee mug in front of her and filled it with an aromatic blend. "You need cream, hon?"

Tobie reached for the sugar dispenser. "Yes, please, and a menu."

"If you're eating breakfast, just tell me what you want. We'll cook about anything."

This was simple. "Two eggs over easy, four slices of bacon, and—if I'm still far enough south—I prefer grits instead of hash browns." She glanced over at another customer's plate. "And a couple of biscuits smothered in sausage gravy."

"Breakfast of champions," the waitress said, scribbling the order, then slapping it down in the long pass-through to the kitchen.

She turned back to Tobie. "Haven't seen you around here before, but judging from that fancy truck you parked outside, you must be the hauler who lost a racehorse in the storm."

Tobie sipped her coffee, savoring the smooth brew. "I guess it's the biggest gossip going around town."

"Well, Ricky has been asking everybody to keep a lookout for it."

She realized that the low hum of chatter around her had quieted. She raised her voice so all the ears turned toward her could hear. "I appreciate that, but please tell everyone there is no reward for her. I don't want a bunch of guys trying to run her down with their four-wheelers. If they got her hurt, the company that insures her would surely sue for damages. And trust me, she's worth a lot of money to them."

A white-haired man sitting two seats away held out his cup for Cindy to refill and spoke up. "How else you going to catch a horse that can run that fast?"

"She's used to people taking care of her. I only need to get close enough for her to see a grain bucket, and she'll probably come right over."

"Order up," a gravelly voice called from the kitchen, and Cindy served up Tobie's steaming breakfast.

A man from the booth behind her spoke up. "You going to drive that fancy truck out in the foothills?"

Tobie tucked into her breakfast but answered between bites. "I heard there was a dude ranch about forty-five minutes from here. I thought I'd go over there and see if I can rent a horse from them, and maybe a smaller trailer to haul it."

"That's a good plan," Cindy said. "They're nice people."

"There's a lot of ground to cover. That horse could be any-where," another man said.

"I figure I'll start out where she first ran off and see if I can track her."

"Good luck with that," a woman from another booth said. "There's so many of them wild horses out there, you'll see tracks all over."

She washed down a big bite of biscuit and gravy with a swallow of coffee. Damn, that was good. "Yeah, but my horse is wearing shoes. It'll be easy to tell her from the others."

"You should talk to Wild Maggie," Cindy, the waitress, said, with half the diner customers nodding in agreement. "She's got trail cameras all over the place to keep up with the wild horses... practically lives with them."

This woman again? She must be infamous in this area. Tobie pictured a woman hermit with crazy eyes and long, frizzy hair sticking out in all directions, like something out of a low-budget movie. Still, if she had trail cameras out there, it might be helpful to take a look at them. "How do I find her?"

Cindy pointed east. "Drive that way out of town, and you'll see a black mailbox with a horse rearing up. That's her place."

"Better make sure she knows you aren't one of those government guys," the man sitting next to her said loudly, drawing chuckles from several others.

"I heard the last time those BLM boys went on her property, she got her shotgun after them and filled their butts with rock salt, then shot out the headlights on their truck," another diner said.

"That story gets bigger every time you guys tell it," Cindy said, grabbing another filled order and delivering it to the customers in the booth at the far end of the counter. "Ricky said she only threatened to shoot 'em."

"They ought to make dog food out of all those horses. That's all they're good for. Ranchers need that grazing ground to raise beef cattle to feed hungry Americans." The big man sitting in the corner had been silent, but his deep voice now rose above the ongoing conversations. "She's fighting a losing battle. As soon as the right people get control of Washington, they'll round up the rest of those pests and ship them off to slaughterhouses in Mexico."

Tobie had seen news reports of the battle between ranchers and wild horse enthusiasts for the rights to graze on federal lands, but she'd never given it much thought because she was focused on building a business hauling horses. "I don't intend to get in the middle of that fight," she said. "I just want to retrieve my horse and be on my way."

"Then go see Wild Maggie," the man sitting closest to her said.

Tobie slugged down the last of her coffee and slapped enough money onto the counter to cover her breakfast and a generous tip. "I might if I don't have any luck on my own."

She gave Cindy a thumbs-up. "Great breakfast. Give my compliments to the cook."

She stopped on the edge of town to refill her truck with diesel, and a man filling his old Ford on the next pump sauntered over.

"You're that woman looking for the lost horse?"

Tobie figured she must be the only fresh news in this little town. "That's me."

He lifted his ball cap to scratch his buzz cut. "How you gonna catch a racehorse? Looking to corner it somewhere?"

"Nope. Gonna lure her with a bucket of sweet feed when I find her." How many times was she going to have to explain this?

He nodded. "That might do it. If you can find her. Lots of country out there."

"I should be able to track her."

"You should go see Wild Maggie. She could help you find your horse."

The gas pump clicked to indicate her tank was full. "Thanks. That's already been pointed out to me." Tobie gave a quick wave and climbed back in her truck. Tired of having this conversation over and over, she was beginning to resent this woman she'd never even met.

Maggie parked her semi over the granary's metal grate to unload her last trailer full of sorghum. It'd been a good harvest this year, and she was happy to be cashing in at a good rate. She climbed out of the cab to watch workers open the hoppers on the underside of her trailer. She loved watching the grain pour from the trailer and sift through the grates, where the first of a system of conveyor belts transported it through a sorting chamber to get rid of small debris, then into a drying silo. She never tired of marveling at the ingenuity of farm machinery.

When the trailer was finally empty, she went into the office to settle up with the granary manager.

"Hey, Dusty. How's the wife and kids?" It was impolite not to ask in a town so small that most everybody knew everyone.

"Everybody's fine. My oldest is starting high school this year. It's driving me crazy that she already has boys sniffing after her."

Maggie laughed. "Fathers always worry about their daughters."

Dusty shook his head. "I remember too well how girls were all me and my friends could think about at that age." He checked his computer, punched in some numbers, then printed out a receipt for her. "You want a check or a direct transfer to your bank?"

"That was the last of it." She took a quick look at the paper he handed her, smiling at the dollar total. "You can just send it to my bank account." She folded the paper and tucked it in her back pocket to leave.

"Hey, you heard about that woman who lost a horse in that pileup they had out on the highway the other day?"

Maggie sighed. Didn't people have anything else to talk about? "Yeah. I heard."

"Since your harvest is done, you could probably help her find it."

She shook her head. "I've got sorghum fields to turn over and lime to put down in my pastures."

"Lots of people got a good second cutting off their hay fields, and a couple say they're going to get a third because we had so much rain this year."

"Much more and we'll all be planting rice in the flooded fields."

"You've still got time to put up a second cutting of hay."

"I've already baled and put up my first cutting. I always leave the rest for the wild horses to graze in winter when things get tough in the foothills."

"I heard Ricky feels real bad that he let that lady's horse get away. You most likely could find it for him in just a day or two."

"Not my problem. That mare will probably take up with a wild herd and be fine. I'm sure that hauler has insurance that'll pay for the loss."

"I reckon so," he said. "See you around."

She waved her good-bye and headed back to the farm. Maybe she'd take another ride out just to check on the runaway mare. But she had no inclination to catch it.

Chapter Seven

A ponytailed woman in a red flannel shirt leaning on the porch railing stood and watched when Tobie parked her truck at the main building of the dude ranch.

"Hey," Tobie said. "Is the boss around?"

"Yep," the woman said. "That would be me." She held out her hand and introduced herself.

Tobie accepted the handshake. "Tobie Mason. I called earlier about renting a horse and small trailer from you."

"I figured that was you. Come on in, and we'll sign some papers on the horse and trailer." She opened the double oak doors that led into an impressive lodge. "You can't spit in that town without hitting someone talking about your expensive racehorse running loose. Aren't you worried someone else might catch it and sell it in the next state?"

"Wouldn't do them any good without her registration papers, proving her pedigree."

"I don't know. One of these cowboys could take her to some backwoods tracks and win some money off her if she's fast enough."

Tobie didn't want to consider that scenario. "I guess that could happen, but they have to catch her before I do."

"Good luck." The woman pushed a lease agreement across her desk for Tobie to sign. "This is a standard agreement, paying per day for one horse and a two-horse trailer since you can't say how many days you might need it."

"I appreciate you accommodating me."

"Well, kids are back in school, so we're not fully booked. I'm going to lease Muddy to you. He's one of our fastest and strongest horses." She eyed Tobie. "I know you haul horses, but I'm guessing you're an experienced rider, too?"

"Rode my first pony at the age of six."

"Okay, then. Let's go get you hitched up."

Tobie expertly backed up to fasten a well-used two-horse trailer to her truck, then loaded the reddish-brown gelding the woman led out of the barn.

"I went ahead and saddled him for you since I figured you wanted to get out looking right away. I put a couple of hay bales and some feed in the second stall, along with his halter and lead rope. You should be all set."

"I hope to have him back to you in a couple of days."

"Keep him as long as you need him."

Tobie had started to climb back into her truck when the woman stopped her. "You know, you might could find that horse a lot faster if you check in with Wild Maggie. She pretty much knows where every horse in three counties is grazing these days."

"You're about the tenth person who's recommended her." She was impatient to get on her way, but her curiosity had been nagging at her. "Why do they call her Wild Maggie? Is she crazy or something?"

The woman laughed. "Not at all. She earned the nickname because she's the self-appointed guardian of a handful of wild horse herds in this part of the state."

"So she's not some eccentric hermit who lives out on the plains with the horses?"

"I think she camps out a night or two just for fun, but the Wild label comes from her concern for wild horses. She's salt-of-the-earth and related to half the people in this town. Google Maggie Wilkes and check out her website."

"Maybe I will."

❖

It was near noon when Maggie set out with Penny and Kate to check her far pastures for signs that horses were already grazing on the new hay sprouting up. The sun was bright and burning off the morning's chill, but the hint of crisp mountain air lingered. She absolutely loved being outdoors with just the scent of pine forests, the creak of saddle leather, and the rich aroma of horse. Kate trotted along beside them, tongue lolling and a wide dog grin on her face. Only a flock of sheep to herd could make her happier.

To an outsider, this part of the state might look like muddy farms surrounded by fields of scrubby grass clumps, cactus, and rocks, leading up to heavily wooded foothills. To Maggie, it was a paradise of wildflowers, succulent grasses, clean air, and abundant wildlife. Her six years away at college, living in a city, had been torture. Out here, even the desert areas were beautiful in her eyes.

She hadn't ridden far when she spotted the black stallion, Night, and his family of five mares and three youngsters. Standing tall with his head raised, he snorted, letting her know he'd seen and scented her. She reined Penny to a stop and ordered Kate to lie down. She'd observed them for hours like this many times, so Night recognized she wasn't a threat and turned his attention to something on her right.

Maggie followed his gaze and stilled. The mare was grazing a short distance away, still wearing her halter and dragging her lead rope. This could be dangerous, she knew. A predator like a wolf could grab the leather halter and drag her down, or she could step on her own rope while running and send herself into a headlong tumble.

She whistled softly, and the mare raised her head to find the source of this human sound. Maggie dismounted when the mare spotted her and freed a collapsible bucket from her saddle bag before filling it with grain from the other side. "So, you are Sarah's Heart," she said softly, holding out the bucket. "How about some tasty sweet feed?"

Heart's ears flicked forward, and Maggie grabbed a handful of the grain, letting it pour from her hand back into the bucket to release the scent of molasses in the air. Heart bobbed her head and took a tentative step in her direction. "That's it, girl. Come on over so I can get that halter off you."

She had no intention of hauling this horse back to the life of a racer, especially since Night's herd was letting her graze so close to them. It was a tentative indication of acceptance. She shook the bucket in repeated invitation, and Heart dutifully walked over to her like any horse accustomed to being fed by humans and buried her nose in the bucket.

Maggie unbuckled the halter and let it drop to the ground when Heart raised her head again to watch her surroundings while she munched a mouthful of grain. She rubbed the mare's neck. "You are a beauty," she said softly. Except for some twigs tangled in Heart's mane and tail, she looked fine after two nights in the wilderness. Maggie checked Heart's feet to make sure no stones had lodged under the horse's shoes. She made a mental note to bring her hoof nips next time to pull those metal shoes from Heart's hooves. When Heart finished the grain, she wandered toward the other horses and began to graze again.

Night watched intently, snorting and prancing closer while Maggie packed up the bucket and Heart's halter and lead line, then remounted. She moved away a short distance, and Night trotted over to Heart. They touched noses for a moment, and then he began grazing alongside her, placing himself between Heart and Maggie. She smiled at his clearly possessive move. This horse was going to be fine with him.

Tobie parked her truck and the two-horse trailer at an abandoned gas station about a mile from where the accident had happened and unloaded the gelding she'd leased. Like most of the horses in this area, he was a quarter horse—built for sprinting but not distance running. No matter. She didn't plan to catch Heart by chasing her.

She secured her saddlebags filled with grain and first-aid supplies in case Heart was injured when she found her. She mounted up and touched her heels to the gelding's side. "Let's go, Muddy."

It didn't take long to reach the accident scene. The deep ruts that had mired her trailer were dry and hard now, and the roadside was still littered with shards of glass and metal. She steered Muddy clear of the debris and raised her field binoculars to scan the area. Nothing was moving except a curious prairie dog watching her watch him.

It was near noon, and the sun was warming the earth around

her, while a gentle wind carried the scent of pine and wildflowers under a cloudless blue sky. She filled her lungs with it. She didn't regret working so hard to establish her hauling business, but she missed having time to mount up and disappear into the woods with a bedroll, a canteen, and a few cans of beef stew. The beauty of the woods, the scent of horse sweat, and the peace of solitude were her happy place.

The storm had washed away most of the hoof and boot prints, but the evidence that her other two horses had been tied in the thicket was obvious. Half-eaten leaves and grass, a pile of horse manure, and some faint hoof prints dotted the area, but before she made it all the way to the trees, a line of deeper tracks veered off into the open plain. The depth of the prints in the sandy soil and the spacing clearly indicated a horse that was running.

Tobie followed the tracks as far as she could, but the trail stopped when she reached a rockier terrain. She lifted the field glasses and again scanned ahead in the direction she'd been tracking. Not even the prairie dog was nearby now, so she gambled that the mare didn't change direction and urged the gelding forward.

She hadn't ridden long when she came across more horse signs, but these were different. Instead of following the trail of a single horse, the ground was suddenly a collage of unshod hoofprints. If Heart had joined this herd, Tobie couldn't pick out her hoofprint from the others. It appeared the herd had stopped there and milled about before continuing. After scouting the area, she decided all the horses had left together. No shod tracks led away from the group, but she followed. Horses were herd animals, and she was counting on that instinct to have influenced Heart to join one of the wild groups. They would, at the very least, show her where to find water.

❖

Maggie stared into her freezer, then shuffled things around in her pantry. Crap. She hated buying groceries, but she'd depleted her supply of frozen and canned dinners. It wasn't that she didn't know how to cook. She just found it inefficient to cook for one person. That usually meant she had to eat the same thing for several days or waste food by throwing out the leftovers. Maybe she needed to get a few pigs to eat her leftovers, so they didn't go to waste. The chickens would eat some of what she threw into their pasture, especially rice and grits, but not everything.

She slammed the door to the pantry closed. Not even a slice of bread. She did have plenty of fresh eggs, but she'd eaten them scrambled for the past three days, due to her shopping avoidance. She sighed. She sure didn't want to be hungry when she bought groceries, and she was very hungry. The eggs she'd eaten that morning were long gone from her stomach, and she'd skipped lunch while she was out tracking horses. Not to mention that it was beef stew night, one of her favorites, at the diner.

She poured out some kibble for Kate, then grabbed her truck keys. "Keep an eye on things, girl," she said to the dog. "I'll be back in a couple of hours."

Tobie scraped the bottom and sides of her bowl to shovel in her last spoonful of beef stew. "Damn, that was good," she said to Cindy, the waitress.

"I can get you another bowl, hon," Cindy said, smiling at the speed with which Tobie emptied the generous bowl of stew.

Tobie rubbed her belly. "I don't think I could stuff another bite in right now, but you can fix me up another serving to go. And a half dozen of those fluffy biscuits, too."

"You got it," Cindy said, refilling Tobie's coffee cup before scribbling down the order and placing it in the window for the cook. "Any luck finding your horse?"

Tobie shook her head. "Not really. It appears she joined up with a wild herd."

"Oh, dear."

"No, really. That's good. They'll show her where to find water and the best grazing. And a herd is easier to track than a single horse."

"That's why you should talk"—the door swung open as a new customer came in—"to her." Cindy waved at a slender woman dressed in jeans and a faded flannel shirt. "Hey, Maggie. Come sit over here. I've got someone who wants to discuss your horses."

The woman moved with athletic grace as she walked over and slid onto the counter stool next to Tobie. "They're not mine or anyone else's horses, Cindy. They're wild."

Cindy waved her hand in the air dismissively, then plunked down a glass of ice water in front of Maggie. "Maggie, this is Tobie. She's looking for her lost horse and thinks it might have joined up with one of the wild herds."

Tobie instantly recognized the intense blue eyes that seemed to evaluate and calculate everything they scanned. Those eyes had crept into her thoughts from time to time. She held out her hand. "We met when you pulled my rig out of the mud but were never properly introduced. I looked for you afterward, but you'd left before I got to thank you."

"I'm always happy to help out," Maggie said, giving Tobie's hand a quick but firm shake, then smiling briefly when Cindy placed a bowl of stew and a basket of four biscuits in front of her. She tucked in to her dinner without further conversation.

Tobie buttered another biscuit and watched her eat for a minute or two before prodding her. "So, everyone tells me that you monitor the wild horse herds in the area."

"Yep."

"I know you're aware that one of the horses I was hauling escaped during the storm."

"Yep. My nephew, Ricky, feels bad about that." Maggie continued to eat without looking up.

"I think my mare might have taken up with one of the wild groups. Have you seen her around? She'd stick out because she's sixteen hands, and the mustangs tend to be around fifteen, a good bit shorter. She's a bay with white on her forehead and one white foot."

"I don't have your horse."

Tobie blinked in surprise. "I wasn't accusing you. I was wondering if you'd seen her around, or on the trail monitors everybody says you have in the places where the mustangs frequent."

"Found a halter and lead line in the brush. I have it in the truck. It might be yours."

"Great! Can you show me where you found it?" Tobie opened a map app on her phone. "I'll start searching there tomorrow morning."

"Not sure I remember exactly where I ran across it."

What the hell? "I only need the general vicinity." Tobie pushed her phone across the counter, next to Maggie's plate. "Just give me an idea where you were when you found the halter."

Maggie stopped eating and finally turned to Tobie. "If she's been accepted into one of the herds, why not just let her be free? I'm sure a horse like that was insured."

"Yes, but by my hauler's insurance. They might cancel me if I don't recover that horse and they have to make a big payout. At the very least, they'd raise my rates sky-high."

"Maybe you should sue the kid that caused the accident. His insurance might be liable."

"Already checked that. Since he didn't directly hit my rig, they won't accept responsibility. I guess I could sue in civil court, but that would take more time and attorney fees than I'm willing to gamble on a long-shot case."

Maggie shrugged. "Just a suggestion." She turned back to her stew.

Tobie's frustration was about to boil over. She was tired, sore, and dirty from riding the fields all day. "You aren't being very helpful for someone who is 'always happy to help out.'"

Maggie put her spoon down and turned back to face Tobie. "You want me to help you send that horse back to a racetrack where she'll spend twenty-two hours of the day in a stall so she'll be crazy to run once she's let out on a track? Where she'll run until her heart bursts from exertion or illegal drugs or her leg breaks because she was put on a racetrack before her joints were fully developed?"

"For your information, that mare is five years old and finished with racing. She's being retired to a breeding farm, where she'll have a warm stall at night, two meals a day, and large pastures to run and graze."

"And what if she turns out to be a poor breeder? She'll be sent to auction or, even worse, a slaughter sale."

"That's not going to happen."

"You don't know that for sure."

"And what if she colics because she doesn't know what plants she shouldn't eat in the wild?" Tobie asked. "Or she starves during the first bad winter? Or what if she's killed by a bear or a pack of wolves?"

"Not going to happen," Maggie said, jutting out her chin.

"You don't know that." Tobie turned Maggie's words back on her.

"Well, I reckon she should be able to outrun any bear or wolf pack. Her life might be shorter out there, but at least she'll die free."

"Hey, hey." Cindy plunked down Tobie's takeout order next to her. "You guys are getting a little loud. Everybody in the place is wondering if you're going to start slugging it out."

Tobie stood. "My apologies. Everybody in town has been telling me to ask Wild Maggie for help, but it seems she doesn't want to help me. No worries. I can find my horse myself." She tossed thirty dollars on the counter and grabbed her takeout order. "Keep the change."

❖

Maggie stared after Tobie as she exited the diner, then turned back to Cindy. "Seems she doesn't need my help."

"You can be such an ass sometimes, Maggie." Cindy cleared Tobie's plate and wiped down the counter for the next customer.

"I never said I'd help her, and it's not my fault everybody else thought I would. The horse has already found a new family, and her stallion is a good one. He'll take care of her."

Cindy turned on her, hand on her hip. "You already know where her horse is." It was a statement, not a question. "I swear, Maggie Wilkes. You don't just act like an ass. You are one."

Only Cindy could talk to her like this. They had a history. They'd been lovers when they were much younger, but their parting had been mutual, and Cindy had since married a man and had three children.

"I'm not being an ass. If that horse really wanted to be caught, she'd already have turned up at someone's barn. But if she wants to live the rest of her life wild, then she should be left alone."

"It's not your horse, so not your decision," Cindy said.

"I'm saying it should be the horse's decision. Not mine, and not that hauler's." It was time to change the subject. "Can I get some coffee?"

"No." Cindy, of course, wasn't finished scolding. "You don't deserve coffee."

"For Christ's sake, Cindy. I'm a paying customer."

"Whatever." Cindy grudgingly slid a mug her way and filled it with hot brew before making the rounds to refill drinks for other customers. She returned as Maggie was using a biscuit to mop up the last of her beef stew and picked up the conversation as if she hadn't walked away. "I thought you'd be nicer to her just because she's the hottest woman to stop in our little town since Parker Dean left for college."

Maggie pretended to concentrate on spreading grape jelly on her last biscuit. "I hadn't noticed."

Cindy snorted. "Yeah, right. Don't forget I know your looks, and I saw you looking." She leaned close and lowered her voice. "And she was wearing your favorite horse-sweat cologne." She sniffed. "Smelled kind of like you do."

"You're crazy." Okay. So, the hauler was attractive—tall, with a short, shaggy cut of sun-streaked blond hair and velvet-brown eyes.

"Uh-huh." Cindy peered past the diner's mostly glass front at the parking lot. "Is that Melissa she's talking to now?"

Maggie whirled in her seat and narrowed her eyes. Melissa Upton was the town's sleep-with-anybody blonde. Not that she cared who Tobie might be talking with, but somebody should tell her about Melissa. "Someone should warn her to get all her vaccinations up to date before taking up with the town whore."

"That wasn't nice. Melissa gets around, but she isn't a prostitute. Anyway, I thought you didn't notice or care about the hauler."

Maggie turned back around. "Don't care. She can hang out with whoever." She threw money on the counter and gulped down her last swallow of coffee. "I gotta go buy groceries," she said.

"Well, that explains your grumpiness," Cindy called after her. She poured more coffee for a man also sitting at the counter. "I swear, that woman hates grocery shopping more than anything," she told him. A few of the other customers nodded in agreement with her observation.

CHAPTER EIGHT

Tobie strolled down the unfamiliar grocery aisles searching for the items on her list. She was dead tired and looking forward to climbing into her bed. She'd bedded Muddy down in her fancy trailer, where he'd have plenty of room to move around, and he'd been enjoying his evening meal when she left to search for her own because her pantry was empty.

Fast food was limited in this little town, but she had grown tired of the usual burger chains after years on the road. She did enjoy breakfast—the most important meal of the day—at whatever diner was around, but she was happier when she could heat a favorite frozen dinner or a can of soup for dinner. She did have a full-size refrigerator so usually stocked up on frozen dinners. They cut down on cleanup after she'd eaten. A couple of cans of biscuits, eggs, a loaf of bread, and some lunch meat rounded out her menu. Her needs were simple. Oh, and coffee. Couldn't forget coffee.

"Excuse me."

She was pondering the coffee offerings when a familiar voice behind her startled her. She whirled, then relaxed in relief when she stared into sky-blue eyes. "Sorry." She moved her cart to the side to allow Maggie to pass.

"Am I that scary? You looked like you were about to leave your groceries and run."

Tobie could feel the flush of heat in her neck and cheeks. "Not you. I was afraid that handsy woman from the diner parking lot had followed me here."

"Ah. Melissa. Better have all your shots if you're going to tango with her."

Tobie stared. "Not planning to do anything with her, but thanks for the warning." She moved closer to whisper, "Is she a prostitute?"

Maggie chuckled under her breath. "If she got paid for sleeping around, she'd probably have a cool million tucked away somewhere. But no, she's not a prostitute. Just an indiscriminate nymphomaniac."

"You're saying she'll fuck anything?" Tobie eyed Maggie. She wasn't sure if this comment was a helpful warning or a snide comment about the woman choosing her to hit on.

Maggie coughed like she'd swallowed her tongue. "Not anything, but maybe anyone," she said once she found her voice again. "No reflection on you," she added.

Tobie watched her take a deep breath, then clear her throat.

"I'm afraid we've gotten off on the wrong foot." Maggie offered her hand. "I'm Maggie Wilkes, local farmer and wild horse supporter."

Tobie hesitated, searching those blue eyes for sincerity, then took her hand. It was warm, soft in spots and callused in others. "Hi. I'm Tobie Mason. I own a business transporting horses and, occasionally, prime livestock."

"I still have your horse's halter and lead rope in my truck, if you want to get them when we leave."

"Sure. Thanks." Several of the coffee brands were unfamiliar, but Tobie spotted her favorite and tossed it into her shopping cart. "That's it for me."

"I've got a few more things to pick up if you don't mind trailing along."

"Lead on."

Tobie added some carrots, apples, and sweet cherries to her cart while Maggie practically filled her own with vegetables and fruit as they browsed through the produce aisles.

"Are you vegetarian?" Tobie asked. "'Cause if you are, I hate to tell you there was beef in that stew we had at the diner."

"You're funny." Maggie's brief smile transformed her face. "I'm not a vegetarian. I just don't eat a lot of meat. I believe in the circle of life, and that includes animals raised to feed humans…as long as those animals are pasture-raised on organic fields and not shot full of hormones to fatten them faster." She placed six bunches of celery in her grocery cart. "And a lot of this is for the animals on my farm. They've just about depleted my summer garden." She carefully added two large watermelons to her stash. "In fact, I'll probably turn the chickens and goats loose in there to finish off what wasn't worth harvesting."

"No apples? Do you ever take some of these treats to the wild herds?"

"Nope. If you feed wild animals—like bears, deer, or raccoons—then you have to deal with the consequences. Bears will rip your door off if they learn there's food inside. Deer will pick your garden clean before the plants have a chance to grow. Raccoons, although cute, are incredibly destructive."

Tobie couldn't believe this woman who was chatting away about vegetables was the stoic woman-of-few-words from the diner. She was a little embarrassed when she looked down at her own cart of frozen dinners and sandwich fixings. "I live out of my trailer and have limited cooking and storage space."

"I don't really buy a lot from the grocery store. I shop for apples, corn, peas, and beans by the bushel from the local farmers' market and put up a lot in the freezer. Or sometimes, I trade for what I need. I raise sorghum and harvest the grain to sell. The stalks are good fodder for livestock but poison for horses, so I trade them for meat that I'm sure was humanely slaughtered."

"My grandmother always had fresh vegetables on the dinner table. I miss that type of cooking sometimes."

Maggie stopped her browsing and turned to Tobie. "No roots anywhere?"

"Not since my grandmother passed away. She raised me after my parents died in a car accident when I was twelve."

"I'm sorry."

Tobie shrugged. "It was okay. I loved my parents, but they were city people with important careers. I hated the city and just wanted to hang out with Grandma in the country. She was an equine veterinarian in Kentucky. She wasn't a warm person, but I spent every summer with her from the time I was six. Her connections were invaluable when I decided to start a business hauling show horses."

Now who was running off at the mouth? Maggie couldn't possibly be interested in Tobie's life story. They cashed out and took their groceries to their trucks.

Clouds had rolled in and obliterated the stars and three-quarter moon so that the parking lot lights were small halos in the pitch-black night. After stowing her groceries, Tobie walked over to Maggie's truck, which could use some body repairs and a fresh coat of paint. Maggie was loading the last bags into her back seat. She reached in and retrieved Heart's halter and lead line, then handed it over.

Tobie frowned, a thought nagging at her. "You must have seen her. How else would you know this was her halter? Anybody could have lost a halter out there."

"Well, I doubt there's another one of these wandering around here." She pointed to the metal plate engraved with *Sarah's Heart* attached to the cheek of the halter.

"Oh. Right."

"Look," Maggie said, glancing around the near-empty parking lot. "I'm sorry about my attitude at the diner. Cindy said I was being an ass, and I guess I might have been."

Bemused, Tobie decided to needle her a little. "Really? I mean, you barely said two words to me when you pulled my trailer back onto the roadway. Then you gave me the cold shoulder at the diner, so I figured you were just naturally ornery."

Maggie frowned and glared at her. "Maybe I am."

Tobie laughed. "No. Just easy to tease." She caught Maggie's arm when she slammed the truck door. "Hey, wait. I wasn't trying to piss you off." She ducked her head to catch Maggie's gaze. "You were starting to lighten up, and I was hoping to draw another smile from you. You have a very attractive smile." She slapped her own forehead. "God. That sounded like a male pickup line, didn't it? I can't believe those words came out of my mouth. I'm so sorry." She felt her face flush as she backed away and was about to turn toward her truck for a quick escape when Maggie's smile stopped her. "Wait. Is that another one?"

"Yeah, yeah." Maggie shook her head, still smiling. "Get out of here." She turned away and started to circle her truck to the driver's side.

Tobie put her hands up in a mock defensive gesture even though Maggie was no longer watching her. "Going. You don't have to get your shotgun after me. A couple of guys I met said rock salt really stings."

She stopped, her blue eyes silver under the streetlights. "Damn right, it does."

❖

Maggie scooped another couple of tomatoes from the pot of scalding water and set them on the table to cool before she skinned and canned them. While the tomatoes cooled enough to handle, she sat at the kitchen table to monitor her trail cameras and return to the bowl of peas she was shelling.

She spent her days outdoors, tracking the wild herds or working her farm. That left only the dark hours for things like cooking and canning. She didn't mind because she didn't like to watch much on television, and she always read for an hour before she went to bed. The solitude and her work kept her centered and the secrets she held safe.

Still, her mind wasn't on her kitchen work tonight. She constantly searched the trail camera feeds for the bay mare, though the image stuck in her head was Tobie Mason—tall, strong-jawed, and with deep brown eyes.

Why had she felt the need to apologize when she saw her in the grocery store? And why did she feel like she'd lied to her, saying she found the halter and lead? Maybe if she'd told her the mare was safe and had joined Night's band...no. Tobie was concerned about her insurance payments, not the horse's freedom. It'd be best to just put that woman and her horse out of her mind.

Movement on the computer screen to her left caught her eye. A group of horses was emerging from the trees onto the meadow where she sometimes camped under the rock overhang. Another group was already grazing the large field, and that group's stallion raised his head to check out the newcomers.

Different groups often cautiously shared favorite watering places or grazed within sight of each other. The few skirmishes between stallions to display dominance rarely resulted in significant injury. The night vision of the trail camera prevented her from seeing details that would identify the herds, but to her practiced eye, the taller mare stuck out like a goose in a flock of chickens. She leaned closer to the computer monitor.

Night, a solid black with no white markings, was invisible in the darkness, but he materialized when Heart grazed too far in the direction of the other herd and their gray stallion took notice. Night challenged him with a show of squeals and prancing, moving between Heart and the gray.

The boss mare of Night's group also took notice. She wouldn't challenge a stallion, but she rounded up her family into a tighter herd and led them a little farther away while her stallion confronted any danger.

Maggie smiled when she saw Night's boss mare, a stocky pinto she'd dubbed Weya, move to graze alongside Heart and subtly guide her deeper into their band. This was good. If Weya, a Sioux word for mother, had accepted Heart, then she was as safe as a horse could be in the wild.

The other stallion answered Night's warning with a display of his own, but neither engaged. There was plenty of meadow for all, and the distant scream of a mountain lion put both on high alert, scanning the forest's edge for real danger.

"Looks like she's settling into life in the wild just fine," Maggie said to Kate. The dog flicked an ear in her direction to acknowledge that she'd heard but didn't look up from her fluffy bed.

❖

Tobie couldn't stop smiling and hummed a tune that stuck in her head while bedding down the gelding. It'd been years since she met a woman who intrigued her like Maggie Wilkes did. She'd never lacked someone to warm her bed if she wanted, but that was happening more and more infrequently. She told herself it was because she'd been so focused on building her business over the past couple of years. Truthfully, her interest in no-strings sex had dwindled as she grew older and more purposeful in her career. She'd begun to feel like dating was too much work and the women were too clingy.

Only once had she made the mistake of letting one woman ride with her on a cross-country haul. Tobie had met her at a bar, and they had great sex almost nonstop for two days. So, she gave in when the woman begged to ride with her. After only three hours on the road, the constant chatter had almost driven her crazy. She'd considered drugging the woman's soda with Dramamine so she'd shut up and go to sleep. Then there were the multiple stops to pee, to get a fresh soda and snacks, or to go inside a restaurant instead of hitting a drive-through. Never again, Tobie had vowed.

Until now. Blue-eyed, standoffish Maggie had piqued her interest. She couldn't put her finger on why, but the attraction was strong. Her interest didn't seem to be returned, but Tobie's libido was ignoring that message.

Her chores finished and groceries put away, Tobie settled into her recliner with her lap board that served as her desk and opened her laptop to google Maggie Wilkes. She found several articles written about her fight with the Bureau of Land Management over their culling of the wild herds to turn more federal land over to ranchers to graze their cattle.

Tobie clicked on the link to Maggie's website and was instantly impressed. The format appeared very professional, including a backstory and a history of wild horses, one page showing the cruel side of BLM roundups and crowded holding pens, where horses might linger for months or even years, bored and separated from their small herd that activists referred to as their family. She nodded to herself. Horse memories were long and friendship bonds strong. She'd witnessed them excitedly greet a friend they hadn't seen for years and grieve the absence or death of a pal.

Tobie admired Maggie's advocacy for the wild herds, but it hadn't changed Tobie's mind about retrieving Heart and transporting her to the breeder who had purchased her. With that thought, she clicked on the website's page that showed Maggie's live trail camera feeds. The cameras were carefully placed so they didn't show landmarks that could give away the horses' location, but she hoped to at least catch sight of Heart and, if she'd taken up with a wild group, study the horses she was running with.

The day had been long, and while she was used to driving for hours, it'd been years since she sat a saddle all day. Her legs and back were already stiffening. She would watch the trail cameras for a while, then take a hot shower before crawling into bed.

Tobie woke with a start at the persistent chiming of the alarm clock on her phone. Damn. She'd fallen asleep in the recliner, and her laptop was warning of a low battery. She moved the recliner into a sitting position and was about to shut the computer down when she saw movement on one feed. Heart was easy to pick out among the other horses, even though dawn was an hour away and the camera was still on night vision. Several horses were drinking from the creek—three pintos, a light-colored horse, and a few darker horses she figured were bays like Heart. She identified a dark shadow in the night vision by his thick neck and alertness as he drank, raising his head often to watch for danger. It was the stallion. The camera feed, however, was no help in locating Heart because the surrounding landscape was too dark to make out any distinctive landmarks…not that Tobie would recognize any.

She closed the laptop, then plugged it in to charge while she took that belated shower to loosen her stiff muscles and readied herself for another day in the saddle. The day's weather report was good, and the horses seemed to be active at night, so she decided to prepare to camp out if she could find Heart's group and needed to wait for an opportunity to get close. Her camp kit was simple—a medium-sized frying pan, multi-utensil tool, a small pouch of seasonings, some instant coffee, water purifying tablets, and a butane lighter. She filled her canteen, then packed the beef stew she'd brought home from the diner and a couple of peanut butter and jelly sandwiches in her saddlebags.

She fed the gelding his morning ration, and since it was still dark outside, she took the time to cook and wolf down several bacon and egg sandwiches while he ate. Always meticulous, Tobie moved the gelding to the small, borrowed trailer and thoroughly cleaned her larger rig of his night droppings, which she bagged for the campground's compost pile, as requested. The sun was just peeking over the distant mountain range when she finally pulled out.

Ricky had given her directions to a property on the edge of the federal lands where she could safely park her truck and trailer while she searched. The state was still winding its way through due diligence to ensure the deceased owner had no heirs before confiscating the land. Just as he had described, the roof on the small cabin had caved in so it was no longer habitable. She spotted a functioning outdoor pump and trough for watering livestock, but the encroaching vegetation left just enough room to turn her truck and the two-horse trailer around when she was ready to leave.

She unloaded Muddy, saddled him, and secured her bedroll and saddlebags. Firearms were illegal in national parks, but Tobie didn't expect to run into a BLM officer on these federal grazing lands, so she carried a handgun holstered on her belt for protection from wildlife and snakes. Her pistol also enabled her to mercifully kill animals injured beyond help and suffering from an encounter with another animal or a vehicle on the nearby highway.

She loved the creak of the leather as she swung into the saddle and the heavy scent of the forest as she followed a deer trail at the back of the cabin Ricky had told her about. She emerged from the woods onto a grassy plain about ten minutes later, and Tobie stopped to survey the area through her small field binoculars. No horse herds were in sight, but she saw several breaks in the surrounding forests that appeared to be animal paths. She touched her heels to the gelding's side and enjoyed his smooth canter as she crossed the field to look for signs that a shod horse had been using those paths.

CHAPTER NINE

Maggie tugged on her work boots and stepped outside. Dawn was breaking and she'd had only a few hours' sleep, but the brisk morning air and the satisfaction of having canned enough tomatoes and put up enough peas to sustain her all winter had invigorated her. She would continue canning and freezing vegetables until the best of the farmers' market summer harvest ended or the local food bank's pantry was full. Rising grocery prices made a lean winter for many families, so she liked to contribute what she could. She hummed an off-key tune as she began the morning feedings and egg-collecting.

The number of feathers on the floor of the coop signaled many of the chickens had begun molting, so she checked the thermostat. Most chickens stopped laying during their molt because their energy went into growing new feathers. They also needed light to lay, and most breeds slowed or quit laying eggs as the days grew shorter. Her hens were prolific producers in the spring and summer, and she kept a handful of breeds that would lay consistently throughout the year. Yet Maggie felt that all the chickens needed to rest from egg-laying while they molted and during the winter, so she didn't use heat lamps like most chicken farmers did.

Always at her heels, Kate carefully searched for eggs that some cantankerous hens would leave in weird places rather than in their nest, picking them up in her mouth and gently depositing them in the basket Maggie set on the floor. When they were done, she rewarded Kate by breaking open one of the eggs and letting her lap up its goodness.

She was finishing feeding the goats when Ricky pulled up in his patrol car.

"Hey, Aunt Maggie," he said. "Mama wanted me to drop by for some eggs."

"Sure. I've got more than enough, but I'm going to send them in a paper bag if she didn't give you some of my cartons to bring back."

"You know she didn't."

"Then you'll just have to be careful. Come on in the kitchen so I can wash these for her."

"Okay." Ricky followed her inside but paused to scan the trail camera monitors. "So, Cindy said you refused to help Ms. Mason find her horse."

"The horse has taken up with Night's group, so she's doing okay. He's a good stallion." She carefully washed each egg in the sink and set it aside to dry. "The way I see it, if she prefers the security of captivity, she'll turn up at someone's barn, looking for a bucket of sweet feed. Right now, she seems to be enjoying her freedom."

"What if she eats the wrong thing and gets sick? What if she gets a hoof abscess because she isn't used to running in fields that have rocks? What if she falls down a ravine in the dark?"

Maggie turned to him, drying her hands on a dish towel. "Why are you so concerned about this one horse? I know you feel responsible, but I've never seen you so worried about someone else's property. What else is going on here?"

"Nothing." He wouldn't meet her gaze at first, but after a moment he snorted and looked up at her. "Did you forget I'm engaged to be married in a few months? Besides, if you're worried that I'm hitting on her, forget it. I might have grown up in a small town, but that woman had gay vibes pouring off her. I'll leave that territory to you." He grinned. "When I had breakfast at the diner this morning, Cindy said you looked that sexy newcomer's way more than once."

"How about we both leave her alone?"

He shrugged but didn't agree.

She narrowed her eyes at him. His fidgeting was familiar. "Go ahead and tell me what news you're about to choke on."

Ricky sat down at the table, scanning the trail monitors again. "It's nothing much."

She waited.

"Okay. So, the insurance company has posted a reward of ten thousand dollars for return of the horse." He straightened his shoulders and looked up at her. "I'm thinking of taking a few days off and heading out myself to see if I can catch the mare."

"You'll never catch her. First, she's too fast for your horse to get you close enough to rope. Second, she's under Night's watch, so you won't likely be able to sneak up on her. Finally, don't you think it will look a little suspicious if you collect that reward since you were the one who set her free?"

He stood quickly, his face reddening and his volume rising. "I didn't free her. I held on while she dragged me through cactus and didn't let go until a big rock knocked me out."

She laughed at him. "Calm down. I'm just telling you what those insurance guys are going to say to try to wiggle out of paying you if you do catch her." Her smile faded as a new thought hit her. "How many people know about this reward?"

He plopped back down in the chair, frowning at the monitors. "Everybody, if loud-mouth Beth has anything to do with it." His face puckered in an expression of distaste.

"How did Beth find out?" The young blonde, hired to be the department's dispatcher right after completing high school, was Sheriff Clark's daughter and the worst gossip in town.

"The insurance company sent a notice of the reward to the sheriff's department, and Beth broadcast it to all the deputies. So you can guess what tongues were wagging about at the diner this morning."

She sighed. "Great. Every yahoo in the county is going to be out looking for that horse."

Maggie had decided she wouldn't concern herself further with this mare, no matter if she stayed wild or was caught and returned to captivity. Tobie's strong features and deep brown eyes flashed through her thoughts. Besides, something about that hauler unsettled her, so she was planning to just lay low until she was gone.

But Ricky's news changed everything. Horses and people

would end up getting hurt if every idiot in the county was out chasing the wild horses with their motorcycles and four-wheelers.

She'd planned to spend the day on the tractor, turning the sorghum fields under to prepare for winter. Now she should probably saddle up and go warn the woman she'd decided to avoid.

She placed several dozen eggs in a paper bag and set it on the table next to Ricky. "Take these to your mother, and then have lunch at the diner later on me." She gave him ten dollars from her wallet. "While you're there, I want you to drop some hints that the mare has been seen outrunning a pack of dogs near where the highway crosses the state line."

He frowned, scanning the monitors again as if he might see the horse. "You don't have any cameras that far away."

"It's to throw the idiots off her trail, Einstein." Maggie was always the cool aunt and had a teasing relationship with her nieces and nephews. She had also been an anchor in their lives after her brother-in-law had a fatal heart attack when they were young teens.

His eyes widened. "Excellent idea." He grabbed the bag of eggs. "I'll drop these off for Mama, then head over for an early lunch."

"Slow down, Speedy. It's not even eleven o'clock. Wait till noon, when the diner's full of people."

"Right. Wait till noon." He hesitated at the door. "I know what. I'll drop by the Feed & Seed and plant the idea among those old farmers who hang out there to gossip."

"Excellent." She practically pushed him out the door and walked him to his cruiser. "Take those eggs first. Don't want them getting too warm in your car and hatching out."

He shook his head but smiled. "I quit falling for that line when I was eight years old, but I do plan to use that trick when I have kids of my own."

She closed his car door while he buckled his seat belt. "You've got to get married first so those children you're planning have a last name," she said, still smiling. She tried not to play favorites, but she had a bond with Ricky that was stronger than the others. He'd spent the most time at her farm as a kid and shared her interest in horsey things. "Have you seen the hauler this morning?"

"Ms. Mason? No, but I told her about the old cabin that the state's taking over. I thought she could park her truck there while she looks for her horse. Nobody can see it from the road, so people won't be likely to try and break into it."

Maggie knew exactly where he was talking about. "I was going to turn over the sorghum fields today, but that can wait. Kate and I'll ride in that direction and warn the hauler if I see her." She avoided calling Tobie by name, hoping it would provide some distance and shake the woman out of her thoughts.

"Okay," he said, starting his car. "But I'm taking the rest of the week off to go hunt that ten-thousand-dollar horse."

She gave him a final wave and strode toward the barn—Kate at her heels—to saddle Penny.

❖

Tobie studied the map on her phone. Over the past hour, she'd seen lots of horse signs but had yet to see a hoofprint from a horse wearing shoes. Surely Heart couldn't have thrown all four shoes after less than a week.

She was plodding along, staring up at the gathering clouds. She hadn't seen a storm in the forecast, but late summer showers weren't unusual in her home state of Kentucky. She didn't know about this area where Utah, New Mexico, Arizona, and Colorado came together. The landscape was a weird combination of desert, forests, grassy plains, and mountains, and the variety of environs made the weather as predictable as a teenage girl.

The sound of hoofbeats jerked her from her forecast musings, and she grabbed her field glasses to get a look at the group of horses emerging from a canyon onto the grassy plain she was skirting. The horse in the lead was a stocky black and white pinto, but at her side was Heart, tall and beautiful. She showed no signs of lameness from the rough terrain and didn't appear to have lost any weight in the week she'd been ranging free.

The dark stallion emerged from the trees last, his head high and nostrils flaring as he scanned the open area for any sight or scent of predators. She could tell the minute he spotted her and was surprised he watched her for a few minutes, then began to graze alongside his mares.

She waited a while, then nudged Muddy in a meandering zigzag to ride nearer to Heart. She was nearly close enough to call out to Heart in a normal voice when the irritating buzz of an off-road motorcycle sounded. The horses were instantly alert, the stallion snorting as he sampled the wind. He shook his head and began circling his mares in preparation to run.

When the dirt bike burst onto the grassy field from the same forest trail the horses had taken, the stallion screamed, and the pinto mare wheeled and led the herd in the opposite direction.

"No, no, no," Tobie muttered to herself.

The horses were headed deeper into the open plain where the motorcycle could easily outpace them.

"Stop," Tobie screamed as she dug her heels into Muddy's side. Without a thought, she arrowed forward to intercept.

The biker, their identity concealed by a full helmet, turned their head toward Tobie, then gunned the rugged motocross cycle. Quarter horses are sprinters, and the one she was riding wasn't bred for racing, so he was no match against the biker's mechanical horse.

She cursed under her breath but reined the gelding in and prayed Heart wouldn't be injured in the chase. Raising her binoculars, she watched Heart break away and outpace the herd. The biker pursued, pulling alongside the mare.

Heart stretched out her neck and lengthened her stride but didn't turn away from the noisy motorcycle. Tobie laughed, realizing the mare seemed to be enjoying the race. And she was fast.

Then, in a surprise move, Heart drifted closer to her pursuer and bit his shoulder. The biker lost control and wrecked in a cloud of kicked-up dirt and grass. Thankfully, Heart had somehow managed to avoid the skidding vehicle and raced in a wide circle to rejoin the herd as they disappeared back into the forest.

Tobie trotted over to the figure sitting on the ground and pulling off his helmet. "Are you hurt?" she asked when the young man looked up at her.

"No." He examined the tear in his leather jacket where Heart had bitten him. "Damn horse got a mouthful of my jacket, not my arm." He threw his helmet in frustration. "I was so close."

Tobie scoffed. "How exactly did you plan to catch her?" She pointed to the lariat looped over his other shoulder. "Did you really think you could control your motorcycle and lasso a racing horse? If you had, by some stretch of the imagination, roped her, she would have dragged you off that bike."

He frowned. "She's not a wild horse. She would have stopped."

She laughed. "Tell that to the last guy she dragged halfway across a field this size. He went to the hospital with a concussion from hitting a rock and is still picking cactus needles out of his skin almost a week later." She put a hand on his arm to steady him when he stood. "I'm surprised, though, that the motorcycle noise didn't seem to spook her. She even looked like she was enjoying the race."

He brushed the dirt from his pants and jacket. "Yeah, well, I don't see you having any luck either. You'll never catch her riding any horse from around here." He pointed at her. "I'll get her. That reward is mine."

She pointed back at him. "The *horse* is mine. Or, at least, until I deliver her to the man who paid over eighty thousand dollars for her. Besides, there's no reward offered for her capture."

"Sheriff's department says there is—ten thousand dollars as of yesterday."

Tobie cursed under her breath. The guy in California hadn't waited the entire two weeks he'd promised before reporting her. "That's my insurance policy offering the reward, and I'm the one who'll end up paying it through higher premiums. So, back off. If you injure that mare by going after her, I'll sue your ass."

"Oh, yeah? So, how do *you* plan to catch her?"

"None of your business, but it won't be by chasing her."

A dog barking drew their attention to the border collie.

"Shit," he said. "That's Kate, which means that crazy Maggie isn't far behind." He picked up his motorcycle and swung his leg over it. "I'm out of here." Without waiting for her reaction, he scooped up his helmet, kick-started his bike, and took off so fast Tobie had to laugh.

She removed her ball cap and fluffed her sweaty hair to let the breeze dry it as Kate ran to her, followed by Maggie astride a mule.

"Hello. Come here often?" She laughed to let Maggie know the old pickup line wasn't a serious flirtation. Or was it?

Maggie should have been furious that Tobie and the guy on the dirt bike were trying to catch the mare on her property. Instead, she was irritatingly pleased to have caught up with Tobie. She slowed Penny to a walk as she approached but scowled when she realized she was smiling at Tobie's tease. "I guess I do, since this is the back side of my farm property."

Tobie scanned the unfenced landscape. "Sorry. I thought this was federal land. I didn't mean to trespass."

She shook her head and consciously softened her scowl. "No way for you to know, but that punk who just ran off knew where he was. The sheriff and I have both warned him to keep that dirt bike off my property. He and his friends like to chase the horses on their motorcycles. It stresses the animals, tears up the grass and trails, and royally pisses me off. I promised him a butt full of rock salt next time I caught him back here."

Tobie chuckled. "No wonder he was so hot to get away." Her smile faded as she stared across the field to where the biker disappeared into the woods. "He said there's a reward offered now for anyone who catches the mare."

A light shower began, so they both pulled out rain ponchos. Maggie preferred hers to her duster most of the time because the poncho folded into a small package easily stored in her saddlebags and would drape over her and her saddle to keep everything dry. She could also string it between trees to use as a small tent, or lash it to the roof of a temporary shelter. She noted Tobie's saddlebags and bedroll before her poncho draped over them. "Looking to camp out tonight?"

"I wanted to be prepared in case I spotted Heart and needed to stay out to trail her a bit to get close." Tobie guided Muddy toward where the wild herd had disappeared into the woods.

Maggie followed, and they walked their mounts along in silence until Tobie stopped at the forest's edge, apparently looking for a trail the herd might have taken. "After that idiot on the motorcycle, the herd will be on high alert. I doubt you'll be able to get very close."

"If I can get close enough, I've got a sack of sweet feed I'm hoping she won't be able to resist."

Maggie nodded. "That could work." She nudged Penny past Tobie's mount. "Follow me. I know where they're probably going."

"Are you actually helping me catch her now?"

"Nope." Maggie didn't turn her head to look but could hear Tobie following. Kate was crashing through the underbrush off to the side of them. "I just want to make sure she wasn't hurt when that moron chased her. I do understand the financial consequences, but I still think you should leave her to live out her life with her new family."

"Easy for you to say. It's not your business on the line."

Maggie didn't answer because she was studying the ground. Night's group had changed direction and was heading for the east prairie. "Damn." She'd hoped they would stay on her property.

"What? What's wrong?" Tobie nudged the gelding to move beside Penny.

"They're headed for federal land."

Tobie looked at the ground, as if the hoofprints could explain. "Don't they normally range on federal lands?"

"Yeah, but I can't legally scare off the reward-seekers when they aren't on my property." She guided Penny in the new direction and whistled for Kate to follow. "I have Ricky spreading rumors that your horse has been spotted way west of here, but obviously at least one guy hadn't heard or didn't take the bait. Also, I don't trust that idiot today to be smart enough not to tell everyone in town where he just saw her. That means he'll have lots of competition tomorrow."

"Son of a bitch."

"Yeah." Maggie slowed when they emerged again from the forest. Night's herd was grazing now on a huge grassland that backed up to the foothills of the Rocky Mountains. Storm clouds had gathered while they were in the woods, and a distant roll of thunder drew a soft woof from Kate. "Let's be quiet and circle around. There's a good place to camp on the other side, near the bottom of that mountain."

They walked their mounts casually around the edge of the woods until they were well past the horses, then cut across grassland. Eventually, they reached the roomy overhang stocked with a small pile of dry firewood. Tobie yelped when Maggie kicked at the wood and a small mouse ran out and disappeared into the tall grass.

"Always have to check for critters or snakes before I bed down here." She chuckled. Tobie normally exuded an I've-got-this aura.

To see her jump and squeal because of a mouse was a crack in that smooth and together persona she projected. "You act like you've never seen a mouse before."

Tobie made a disgusted noise. "I've spent my life around barns, so I've seen plenty. It caught me by surprise when it ran straight at me." She visibly shuddered. "Besides, just because I've seen a lot of mice doesn't mean I like 'em."

Maggie studied Tobie—taller than her by maybe three or four inches, broad shouldered and probably lean, but well muscled under that long-sleeved T-shirt and jeans. *Stop it. Stop imagining her body.* Turning her back to Tobie, she began to remove Penny's saddle. "So, how old are you?"

"Wow. If you want to know something, just ask."

Maggie had to hide her smile at Tobie's sarcasm. "That's what I did. How old are you?"

"Thirty-four."

She whirled, dropping Penny's saddle on the ground. "Thirty-four? More like twenty-four. I want to see your driver's license."

"I'm sure that will feel like a compliment ten years from now, but at this point in my life, it sounds more like an insult."

"How is that an insult?"

"It feels like you're labeling me as inexperienced and immature rather than beautifully wrinkle free." Tobie dropped the gelding's saddle next to Penny's, then crossed her arms over her chest and pinned Maggie with a pointed stare. "How old are you?"

She feigned nonchalance, turning calmly away to exchange Penny's bridle for a loose halter. "Forty-two."

Tobie nodded. "Okay."

"Okay?" Maggie slapped Penny's rump to let her know she was free to graze, then turned back to Tobie. "What does that mean?"

Tobie stared at Penny as the mule ambled off to graze. "You aren't going to put hobbles or a drag on her to make sure she doesn't run off?"

"I couldn't get rid of that mule if I tried," Maggie said. "I rescued her from an auction kill pen and have tried to set her loose with a herd of wild donkeys, and later a herd of horses. But she kept turning up at my barn and letting herself inside."

"Really?" Tobie exchanged the gelding's bridle for a halter and lead line.

"I had to put an extra latch on my back door because she kept trying to come in the house." Maggie held out her hand. "I can tie his lead to her halter, so he can't decide to run off with the wild herd."

Tobie handed her horse over to Maggie, and she walked out to tie their two animals together. The gelding showed no interest in the wild horses grazing some distance away, but the dark stallion and Heart were watching them. She walked back to the overhang and spoke quietly to Tobie. "Your mare is watching, so you might want to set out a bucket of grain and see if she'll wander over."

Before Tobie could retrieve her collapsible bucket from her saddlebags, the stallion moved between Heart and their campsite and used his body to turn her back toward the herd. Heart meekly complied and put her head down to graze alongside her new family.

The sky was heavy with rain clouds, and the distant thunder was growing closer, so Maggie quickly arranged their campsite. The overhang was about twelve feet long and six feet deep, as though a large hand had come along and scooped out the stone surface. She placed each saddle and their belongings on either side of the modest stack of wood. They would use them as pillows when they rolled out their sleeping bags. Then she took enough wood from the stack to start a fire in a rock-lined circle that had obviously been used as a firepit in the past. She had barely finished when the shower turned into a downpour. The raindrops were large, but the cloudburst was relatively light compared to the storm a week ago. The ground fortunately sloped upward under the outcrop, so they didn't have to worry about water pooling where they'd be sleeping.

Tobie stood, watching the herd for a few minutes while Maggie started the fire. None of the horses—theirs or the wild group—seemed to care enough about the rain to interrupt their grazing. She wasn't worried about Muddy. Maggie's mule was apparently birthed by a small draft horse and had enough weight to anchor the gelding.

When she turned around, Maggie reached behind the wood stack to bring out a round grate, apparently scavenged from a small grill, and set it atop three rock stacks skirting the firepit. She placed a small kettle of water on the grate, then began shuffling through several packets of freeze-dried meals.

Tobie hurried over to her saddlebags. "I can do better than that freeze-dried meal," she said, holding up a plastic bag filled with the diner's beef stew. "Also, I never ate the two sandwiches I packed for lunch, so I'm happy to share. I can't eat it all, and it'll probably spoil by morning."

"Thanks. I'm fine eating this." Maggie's hungry gaze fixed on the bag of stew belied her refusal.

"That's too bad, because I was hoping I could swap some beef stew and sandwich for one of your meals that will still be good tomorrow."

Maggie seemed to consider that offer, then looked over her selection of meals and tossed her a packet labeled eggs, cheese, and potatoes. "Okay, but I feel like I got the better end of the deal."

"Not at all. I obviously didn't think ahead very well when I planned to possibly stay out overnight." She placed her small frying pan on the grate and poured the beef stew into it to warm, then handed one of the sandwiches to Maggie, who poured a portion of kibble on the ground for Kate. They rolled out their sleeping bags and sat on them as Tobie wolfed down her sandwich. Maggie ate half of hers and gave the rest to Kate.

Tobie ate half of the warmed beef stew, then handed the pan and spoon to Maggie. "I don't have a bowl, but the rest of the stew is yours."

Maggie nodded, accepting her share. "Do you always eat so fast?"

Tobie wiped her mouth on her sleeve. "I'm usually on the road and have a trailer full of horses waiting if I go inside a restaurant, so I guess it's become a habit." She took her cup and baggies of instant coffee, creamer, and sugar out of her saddlebag. "Do you have enough hot water in that kettle to share?"

Maggie nodded around a mouthful of beef stew. "If you have enough coffee to spare." She produced a cup from her saddlebag.

Tobie nodded and spooned coffee crystals into each cup before adding the hot water. "Cream or sugar?"

"Absolutely. I like a little coffee with my creamer."

"Sounds more like a latte."

"Says you. I've got nothing to prove to anyone. I like my creamer and sugar."

They smiled at each other to acknowledge the banter was friendly, not serious.

They sipped their coffee and stared into the flames for a while. Sharing their meal and teasing comments felt surprisingly cozy, despite the hard stone floor of their campsite and the wet-horse smell.

Penny and the gelding had abandoned the grass and edged under the outcrop as much as possible when the rain started coming down in sheets. They shared the bucket of sweet feed Tobie had set out in hopes of luring Heart. Like best friends, Penny would get a mouthful, then lift her head while she chewed so the gelding could get a mouthful and raise his head for Penny to take her next turn. It seemed everybody was sharing tonight.

Maggie finally rinsed out her cup and put it away. Before she settled down, she took a lead rope from her saddlebags and clipped one end to Penny's halter, then tied the other end to a ring that was attached to the stone wall.

"Did you put that ring there?" Tobie asked.

"Yeah. I trust Penny won't run off while I'm awake, but I don't trust that she won't decide during the night that her dry, cozy stall in my barn is a better place to be than with me."

"So, you stay out here often?" Tobie found this curious when her farm was only a couple of hours away.

"I stay out occasionally to observe the horses and collect data."

"Data on what?"

Maggie laughed. "You probably think I'm just some nutty activist."

Tobie smiled. She liked this more relaxed version of Maggie. "Well, people do refer to you as Wild Maggie."

Maggie shrugged and grew serious again, staring out at the darkness. "I have a doctorate in environmental science. I inherited the farm from my father, who inherited it from his father, but I keep it financially afloat by raising organic sorghum and free-range chickens and dairy goats. I also receive a grant through the American

Wild Horse Foundation to study the true effect of the horses on the land."

"Doesn't the Bureau of Land Management study the wild herds?"

"Yes, but the BLM is under the control of politicians, so their data and conclusions can't be trusted."

"You're not just being paranoid?"

"A lot of their reports suspiciously don't match what we see in the field. We have proof that they downplay the damage and cruelty of using helicopters to round up wild horses and lie about the number of horses killed and injured during their drives. Paperwork on any seriously injured horses gets suspiciously lost, and activists have videoed injured horses being loaded into trailers at night as if they're going to a vet, only to be transported instead to a location where they're loaded into tractor-trailers meant for cows and hauled to meat factories in Mexico."

"What about the ranchers' claims that the horses are overgrazing federal lands?"

"It's the cattle that are overgrazing. The US leads the world in beef production—more than China or Brazil. We're also the biggest consumer of beef. The ranchers pay only a dollar thirty-five a month per cow, a fraction of what it would cost them to graze the animals on their own land. I could go deeper into the statistics, but I don't want to bore you."

"No, really, I'm interested. Just to play devil's advocate, would beef ranchers be able to survive financially without the federal grazing lands? If they all bankrupt, then who would feed hungry Americans?"

"I'm not advocating that the ranchers be kicked off federal lands altogether, but the more cows a rancher can raise, the greater his profit. Those that want the wild horses totally removed are looking to increase their herds for profit, not focusing on feeding America. The federal lands can be shared if we focus on the right programs. Right now, we're trying to close the barn door after the horses have escaped. We should be focusing more on controlling their birth rate, not penning and killing them."

"Is being taken down by a mountain lion and eaten any worse than dying in a stampede or slaughterhouse?"

"I think it is. Their terror lasts only minutes if a mountain lion or a wolf pack takes one down. It's the circle of life. They're thirsty, hurting, and terrified for days when they're crowded into livestock trailers and shipped down to Mexico."

"Okay. I get that a lot of unwanted horses, not just from wild herds, end up in slaughterhouses because Americans can't stomach eating animals they consider to be pets. I'm on your side there. I love horses, or I wouldn't have built a career hauling them around in a luxury trailer. But why turn a domesticated horse out with the wild ones where she might get killed by a predator, starve during a drought, or fall prey to a BLM roundup?"

Maggie was quiet for a while, and Tobie let the silence lie between them. Finally, she spoke.

"Imagine that you were barely weaned from your mother when you were suddenly stuck in a stall most of the day unless you were training to jump out of a metal gate and race shoulder to shoulder with other horses. Oh, you were well fed, exercised once a day like a prisoner, and raced every month or so. Finally, you're retired if you haven't broken down on the racetrack because your bones aren't fully developed when they start running you at full speed. No more rigid training schedules and travel from track to track. Then you break free and meet some other horses who do what they want, when they want, and are never confined. Sure, you were headed for a life where you're well fed, get regular vet checks, and never have to look for shelter. There are no more exhilarating races, but no more standing in the stall until you're about to burst to run. But you're forcibly bred every year, and humans manage your pasture time. Which life would you choose?"

"I don't know. The life as a brood mare is pretty good."

"What if you had a sugar mama who said she'd take care of you as long as you birth some babies for her, and she has control over whether you're confined to the house or go out?"

Tobie waved both hands up. "Hold on there. I'm not into having babies for anyone. And I don't think I'd like being a kept woman."

"It would be a good life. You'd live in relative luxury, not having to worry about your next meal or about being out in bad weather with no place to go."

"I don't care. I'd rather be dirt-poor and homeless than some man or woman's toy."

"So, maybe Sarah's Heart doesn't want to be kept either."

It was a rhetorical statement, so silence fell again. Maggie added some sticks to the fire, and they both retreated to their own thoughts, the mesmerizing flames, and the warm crackle of the burning wood.

Tobie mulled this scenario over, reluctant to admit Maggie had a point. But she had to be honest. "I started my own business because I don't like anyone to tell me what to do. I make my own decisions about whether to accept or turn down a job."

The storm finally blew over, and Tobie pulled off her boots to settle into her sleeping bag. Maggie had given her something to think about, but this was business. Heart wasn't really her horse. She belonged to the breeder in California, and if they didn't catch the mare before he filed for payment from Tobie's insurance company, then the insurance company would own Heart if she was caught in the future. Her fate was actually out of Tobie's hands. "Good night, Maggie."

Maggie didn't answer, but Tobie could hear her slipping into her own bedding, leaving room for Kate to snuggle close.

CHAPTER TEN

Tobie woke slowly. Either she was extra tired or the sleeping bag on a rock surface was more comfortable than she'd anticipated. She groaned when she sat up and struggled to her feet to stretch. Nope. Her deep sleep wasn't because the ground was comfortable. Every muscle in her body ached.

She was surprised and disappointed to see Maggie, Penny, and Kate gone, the gelding tied to the ring in the stone wall. She scanned the field. A group of horses was grazing, but none were from the herd that had adopted Heart. The stallion protecting these mares was a stocky pinto—a patriarch, Tobie guessed, because he showed the bite scars of many challenges from other stallions.

Why didn't Maggie wake her? Right. She'd almost forgotten that Maggie didn't want her to catch Heart.

Tobie intended to saddle up right away and track Heart. But it was still very early, and it wasn't like the horses were running from her. They likely had moved to a water hole, then would go to a new grazing spot—maybe the field they were in before the storm.

She stirred the coals of the fire and added some wood. Maggie had left the grill grate in place, so she filled her metal coffee mug with water and set it on the grate to heat. When it began to boil, she poured some of the water into the freeze-dried meal from Maggie's stash and added more water in the cup to prepare some coffee. Then she studied the horses grazing in the field as if she weren't even there. They were probably used to Maggie being around so didn't mind her presence.

The sun cleared the mountains, making the dew-covered grass sparkle like glitter. The sound of the horses cropping at the grass with their teeth and the occasional snort to dispel a fly or a tickling weed was oddly comforting. She could see how someone could be drawn into the romantic ideal of horses living freely. Hell, even those Western movies made her wonder what it'd be like to have to worry about nothing but raising your own food and tending your livestock like they did. But she was too squeamish about slaughtering animals for meat. She loved all kinds of meat, but she wanted to see it either alive or already processed and wrapped in butcher paper.

Tobie rose stiffly and groaned again when she straightened her back. She sure missed the comfortable bed in her rig. She tossed the rest of her coffee into the dying fire and packed everything, placing the fire grate behind the wood stack where Maggie had stored it before. She'd hobbled the gelding and let him graze while she ate breakfast, but now she saddled him, then tied her bedroll and saddlebags to his saddle.

Her movement around the campsite made the pinto stallion become suddenly alert, and he gathered his herd to move them farther away from her.

"Not hunting you, buddy," she said as the group wandered to the eastern end of the huge grassland. She mounted up and began circling westward around the field to find where Heart's group had entered the woods. She didn't see how the horses could be overgrazing the fields because they moved around constantly. She saw hoofprints of three animals wearing shoes—her gelding's smaller quarter-horse hoof, Penny's large light-draft hoof, and Heart's distinctive shoe—but it was impossible to find the direction of their wanderings because their group and the herd currently grazing on the east end of the field had trampled the rain-softened ground.

She urged the gelding into the woods but ignored the tracks and turned in the direction of the old cabin, where she'd parked her truck and borrowed trailer. The bucket of sweet feed hadn't lured Heart, so she needed to adjust her plan to catch the mare. This phase might require more research…and maybe a visit to Maggie's farm. Yeah. For research, of course. The better she understood the wild herds in the area, the greater her chance of catching Heart.

❖

Maggie jogged Penny most of the way back to the farm, wanting to get home for the morning feeding. She'd awakened well before dawn, as usual, and quietly packed up. She wasn't surprised that Night's group had left and another herd was grazing the field. Night's group had moved into the woods when the rain became heavy and, from their tracks, appeared to be headed toward a box canyon nearby, shielded by steep foothills and offering lush grass, tall oaks, and a deep creek at the bottom. The canyon was completely hidden unless you knew the cavern from which a creek spilled into a small waterfall was actually a passage, not a cave.

But it wasn't the horses that her thoughts returned to again and again as she performed the morning chores. She couldn't shake that tall, brown-eyed Tobie from her thoughts. They obviously didn't agree about the future of that mare, but she would concede that if she did recapture Heart, the mare, though she wouldn't be free, would have a decent life as a brood mare. Maggie recalled Tobie startling when the mouse ran from the wood pile and laughed out loud, causing Kate to yelp and leap into the air, even though she didn't know why they were apparently happy. Maggie laughed again at Kate's antics.

"Down, girl. I was just thinking that if that mare stays wild, a whole herd of racehorses might be out there in a few years. They should give those government boys a run for their money."

Kate wagged her tail furiously and barked her agreement.

"I know, right?" She conversed like this with Kate all the time. The dog was super intelligent and always agreed with her. Well, most of the time anyway. "Let's go inside and cook some breakfast, shall we?"

She fried three of the eggs she'd just collected, two for her and one for Kate, along with some bacon, then dished up breakfast for them both. She switched on the television mounted on the wall beside her kitchen table/desk to listen to the morning news, but the trail-camera monitors in front of her drew her attention instead.

Night's group was in the canyon, as she'd expected, and Cloud, the pinto that was Night's sire, was still grazing his mares in the grassland where they had camped the night before. She zoomed in on the overhang. Tobie was still there, stoking the fire and heating water for coffee and breakfast.

When Tobie walked out into the grass and began unbuckling her belt in obvious preparation to relieve herself, Maggie jumped up to refill her coffee cup. She was sure Tobie didn't realize there was a camera in that field, and her face heated at her near invasion of Tobie's privacy. Still, her mind jumped back to the night before— Tobie taking off her rain-soaked flannel shirt to reveal a ribbed tank top tight across a flat abdomen and high, small breasts before donning a sweatshirt and stretching those long legs out by the campfire. Damn. It had been a long time since she'd noticed another woman. Even longer since a woman had invaded her dreams and made her belly clench.

She settled down at the table again and ate her eggs while watching Tobie saddle up and turn the gelding toward the trail where Night and his mares had exited. She noticed her study the ground, then turn in the opposite direction of the canyon where the herd had gone. Was she that bad a tracker, or was she giving up her hunt?

Maggie mopped up the last of her eggs with a biscuit, then scanned the monitors one last time. Tobie was no longer visible, so she turned her attention to the television while she washed the dishes.

"We have a severe weather warning for tomorrow, with high winds and possible tornadoes coming up from the southwest," the local weatherman said, pointing to a map projected behind him. "Just a reminder that emergency officials have designated Patterson High School as a storm shelter. You all know twisters are common this time of the year, and Sheriff Dan Chandler is advising anyone without shelter or those of you living in mobile homes to head to the high school if you hear sirens warning of tornadoes in the area."

"Shit." That explained why Night had taken his mares to the canyon. Animals could sense impending weather, and the canyon would provide protection from the high winds. Maggie put the last dish away and grabbed a hooded sweatshirt. "Let's go, Kate. We need to get those last two fields plowed under before that storm blows in and turns them into mud."

Normally, she'd already have the fields ready for winter and be busy bartering her silage with other farmers for meat and vegetables to put up in Mason jars or the freezer. But the unusually wet autumn and this lost-horse business had put her behind schedule.

She went to the equipment shed, which was actually a metal warehouse, where she stored two tractors and attachments, her semi cab, a grain harvester, a hay baler, and about two hundred bales of hay. Her equipment was pretty much the same her father had used, but she carefully kept up all maintenance and replaced worn parts.

She sighed when she slid back the tall doors and stared inside. She could almost see her father bent over a tractor in the semi-darkness, changing out a gasket or hose. Damn, she missed him sometimes. But then, they had constantly butted heads over the wild horse issue. He sided with the cattle ranchers, complaining that the herds were knocking down his fences and grazing in his hay fields. After he died of cancer, she removed the fences around the far hay fields.

She climbed into the glassed-in cab of the larger tractor, which was already hitched to a six-foot disc harrow, then called Kate to join her.

CHAPTER ELEVEN

Tobie made herself a sandwich and got comfortable in her recliner with her lap board. She opened her laptop and scanned the trail camera feeds on Maggie's website. No sign of Heart or her herd. She chewed slowly while she thought, then googled Sarah's Heart. The search result produced videos of several of her races. "Impressive," Tobie mumbled to herself. She was about to click on the next video when a young woman appeared in the winner's circle with Heart.

"The hood has made all the difference," she was telling the interviewer. "She's very competitive, and we had trouble during her training because she'd bump other horses who challenged her for the lead."

Tobie laughed. She'd been right in suspecting Heart had intentionally dumped that guy off his dirt bike. Still, not a good move. The machine could have hurt the horse. Now Tobie was curious to see if she could find other interviews with Sarah that could possibly offer some information that would help her catch the mare. The search turned up only a few—mostly interviews before and after races—but one was an interview with a prominent racing magazine. She clicked on the web address.

The video interview was done in a news-interview format like *60 Minutes* used, opening with Sarah standing at a white board fence that outlined a lush paddock. She was thin and pale, and she leaned on her portable oxygen tank for support, but her smile was bright and her voice strong.

"I have a rare genetic form of anemia called Fanconi anemia. It's treatable to a point but incurable. At twenty-three, I'd already lived past my life expectancy, and I was tired of hospitals and treatments, but my father begged me to submit to one more bone marrow transplant."

The interviewer filled in the silence when she paused to catch her breath. "You aren't afraid of dying?"

"My mother died when I was ten years old after a drunk driver hit her car. I'm at peace with my inevitable death because I'm convinced I'll see her again in the afterlife."

"Are you a Christian?"

"I consider myself spiritual, but not religious. Christians have a bloody history of killing people who refused to adopt their beliefs. You know, the Christian Crusades. They aren't still killing people today, but too many have twisted that religion to suit their own prejudices and are trying to make laws that enforce their beliefs…in the same way Iran forces Islamic beliefs on its population. So, no, I'm not a Christian, but I do believe there is life after death, possibly even reincarnation."

"You were twenty-three and tired of fighting to stay alive, so you refused further treatment."

Sarah nodded. "I refused until Dad promised he would give me a foal to train if I would try one more bone marrow transplant." She smiled. "He knew that horses are my life. They're honest, while humans aren't. They're intelligent, unlike some people. And they're loyal. Studies have shown they'll recognize people and animal friends after not seeing them for years." She wavered a bit, and a young man brought a tall stool for her to sit on. "Thank you, Kevin," she said.

"Do you need to pause a bit?" the interviewer asked.

"I need to catch my breath." Sarah adjusted the gauge on her oxygen tank.

"So, your father gave you a filly he named Sarah's Heart?"

Sarah smiled and shook her head. "No. He had a colt picked out that was born two days earlier. But when Heart's mother died during the birthing, that little filly fought to stay alive. My father had a fit, but I slept in the barn with her for two days until we found a surrogate mare that would adopt and raise her."

The video cut to an interview with Sarah's father, Leo Carmichael, in his study.

"This wasn't the horse you initially wanted for your daughter?"

"No. I've been lucky enough to have had several top racers. Sarah was so much like her great-aunt, Penny Tweedy, who owned the greatest racehorse of all time—Secretariat—and I wanted her to have a colt with a Secretariat pedigree. I went to the barn to tell her that Aunt Penny was giving her a Secretariat colt, but when I stepped into that stall, Sarah was sitting in the hay next to a foster mare with that filly sleeping soundly in her lap. She looked up at me and said, 'Dad, this is the one. She's a fighter and has captured my heart.' I immediately knew dissuading her was useless." As tears filled his eyes, he paused and took a deep breath. "So, I looked at my daughter and gave in. I said, 'Well, then we'll have to name her Sarah's Heart.'"

When the video cut back to Sarah, some time appeared to have passed. The stool was gone, and she seemed stronger.

"So, do we get to meet Sarah's Heart?" the interviewer asked.

Sarah nodded and smiled. "We just retired her from a very successful racing career, and she's here on the farm." She turned to the paddock and put her fingers to her mouth to emit a low whistle. The pounding of hooves was immediate, and a bay mare with a white star and one white sock thundered up to the fence. She stretched her neck over the fence to press her forehead to Sarah's, and they both closed their eyes for a few seconds.

But Sarah had grown ghostly white, and she ended their greeting. Then she dug a couple of carrots out of her jacket pocket, and Heart snagged them from her hand right away, bobbing her head as she chewed. Sarah laughed at her antics and turned back to the camera and announced, "This is Sarah's Heart. Carrots are her favorite treat."

The picture froze, and a voice-over announced the inevitable news. "Sarah Carmichael passed away less than a month after this interview. She was twenty-eight years old. Leo Carmichael has since suffered a heart attack and is currently selling off his racing stable to go live with his sister."

The program cut back to the interview with Leo in his study. Tears spilled down his face, but this time he didn't try to hide them from the camera. "That last bone marrow transplant was grueling because Sarah was so weak, but when she was finally released from the hospital and that filly was born, she made us help her down to the barn every day. It was the right medicine, because Sarah seemed to grow stronger daily before her disease took over again." He wiped away his tears with a white linen handkerchief. "That mare gave me five more years with my daughter. Sarah was *my* heart."

When the video ended, Tobie was brushing away her own tears, glad no one was around to see what a softie she was. She backed the video up and paused it where Sarah had turned to the camera and said, "This is Sarah's Heart." Staring into the young woman's blue eyes, she saw the same passion she'd witnessed in Maggie's when she talked about the wild horses. But Tobie wasn't a rich horse breeder like Sarah's father and couldn't comply with Maggie's request to leave Heart in the wild.

"Shit." Maggie swore at an ominous *thunk* and stopped her tractor to climb down from the cab. Kate jumped out after her and began hunting for mice or rabbit nests that the harrow might have exposed. A stone the size of a beachball was wedged between two of the steel discs. She glanced up at the clouds gathering overhead. "Just what I need. Only half an acre to finish, and this damned rock is trying to ruin my day." Kate wasn't listening, because she'd found something interesting and was busy digging in the freshly turned soil to get at it.

Maggie sighed again and walked back to the tractor's cab to grab a heavy-duty crowbar she kept there for just this kind of situation. Her fields had been cleared of rocks years ago, but every farmer was prepared for more to work their way topside over the years.

She was strong, but the stone was wedged tight, so she had to try several different angles before it popped loose. She'd switched off the tractor's PTO shaft that turned the harrow's discs but, in her haste, forgot to watch out when the stymied discs were freed. When the stone suddenly came loose, she fell forward, and the two discs that had been jammed turned a few rotations, slicing into her leg and pinning her under the harrow. "Motherfucker." She didn't like to use that word, but she was truly fucked.

She began digging in the soft dirt to try to free her legs but stopped when she saw the deep gash in one of them. It was bleeding freely, but the dirt she was trying to scoop out was causing soil to fall into the open cut. Damn, it was deep. She was feeling lightheaded, but the bleeding slowed after she used her belt as a tourniquet on her leg.

Kate was immediately at her side, sniffing the cut and whining. *I'll rest a minute and try digging again.* That was her last thought before darkness overtook her.

❖

The knock on Tobie's door woke her from an impromptu nap. She rubbed her eyes as the knocking began again. "Hold on. I'm coming." She opened the door to find Brice, the campground's owner.

"Have you been watching the news about the weather?" he asked.

"No. Should I be?"

"A big storm's blowing up. Should hit here tonight or tomorrow. Oklahoma and Missouri are the only places that get more tornadoes than we do, so I'm closing the campground today and heading for Florida."

"You're going to Florida, the state annually devastated by hurricanes?"

"Hurricane season is pretty much over."

"I haven't found my horse yet."

"Sorry, but I'm turning off the water in the bathhouse and getting out of here. I know this is short notice and you've got two trailers to move, so I'll let you shut the gate when you leave if you promise to close the padlock on the gate then."

"I just dumped my tank and refilled it with water earlier today, so why can't I just stay a few more days? I don't need the bathhouse."

"No can do. My insurance won't cover anyone being here without me here, and this storm could do some real damage."

"Where the hell am I supposed to go?" The wind was picking up, and a big gust gently rocked the trailer.

Thunder rolled in the distance, and Brice's gray buzz cut seemed to stand on end. "You've met Wild Maggie, right?" He pointed toward the east. "She's got an equipment warehouse big enough for you to pull your rig in and keep it safe. Probably the small trailer, too. I'm sure she'll take you in. She has a soft spot for horse lovers."

"I don't know. All I've seen is pretty much the hard-ass side of her."

He laughed. "Yeah. She can be that, too." Then he sobered. "At any rate, you need to get that horse out of this trailer and into a barn, even if you have to drive him back all the way to where you got him." He held out his hand. "Give me your phone."

"What?"

"Your phone. I'll pull up her address on your GPS app."

She handed over her phone, and he quickly opened the app and typed in the address before returning it to her. "I'm not being a Chicken Little here. You need to go."

"Okay, okay." She grabbed her waterproof duster and stepped outside. The sky was dark and threatening. The humidity was so high the air felt thick.

Brice wasn't kidding. His bus-style motor home was idling in the campground's main road outside her campsite. He paused before climbing in. "I'm dead serious, young lady. We've had way too much rain this fall, and the ground around the tree roots is soft. It won't take a tornado touching down to uproot a bunch of the big pines in the vicinity."

She gave him a quick salute to indicate her intention to comply, then quickly moved the gelding from her large rig to the smaller trailer. Wind gusts were pushing at her truck and the small trailer when she hit the open road, and she initiated the GPS map on her phone. She definitely needed to get this rented gelding someplace safe, and the dude ranch where he lived was too far away in these strong winds.

Tobie was pleasantly surprised by the iron W Bar Ranch sign that arched over the entrance to a long, well-maintained gravel driveway leading up to a beautiful old farmhouse with an inviting wraparound porch. She pulled next to the house and got out to knock on the door, but Kate ran toward her like a bullet, barking frantically. Tobie put her hands up. "Whoa, girl. You know me, remember?"

Kate wasn't listening. She continued to bark when Tobie stepped up to the door and knocked. When there was no answer, she knocked again and called out. "Maggie? It's Tobie Mason." Still no answer, but Kate surged forward and grabbed her hand. "What the hell?"

As Kate backed away, still barking, Tobie realized the dog wasn't biting at her. She was clearly imploring Tobie to follow her. "What is it, girl? Where's Maggie?"

The dog twirled in circles, then ran to a field where Tobie could see a tractor stopped. Kate paused a few times, turned around, and stared at her, then ran behind the tractor to the large disc harrow. Tobie spied Maggie's still body right away.

"Holy shit. Maggie, Maggie. Oh, Jesus." Maggie's cheek was cool to her touch, but the pulse in her neck throbbed strongly under her fingertips. "Maggie, wake up."

As Tobie called her name, Maggie stirred and struggled up. "Son of a bitch. My leg." She rubbed a dirty hand across her face. "I must have passed out."

Tobie thought she might pass out when she saw Maggie's leg trapped under one of the large steel discs. It had torn through her jeans and into Maggie's calf. "How long has this tourniquet been on?"

Maggie sank back into the dirt. "Don't know, Sherlock. I was kind of taking a nap." Her retort was sharp but her voice weak.

Tobie shook her head. This was one tough woman, but she needed to loosen the belt for a minute to restore blood flow to Maggie's foot. When she did, blood spurted out. Okay. That wasn't such a good idea. She tightened the belt again. "We need to get you to a hospital to clean that out and sew you up."

"Was trying to dig myself out." Maggie's voice was growing weaker.

"Just lie back. I've got this." She began digging out the dirt from under the injured side of Maggie's leg with her hands, and

Kate started digging furiously on the other side. "That's it, Kate. Dig."

They freed Maggie in only a few minutes, and Tobie tugged her from under the plow. She started to pick her up in her arms, but when she felt Maggie's weight, she knew she wouldn't make it all the way to the house. "Where are the keys to your truck? I'll bring it to you. Mine's hooked to the horse trailer."

"Visor on the passenger side. Put your horse in the barn."

"No time. We need to get you to the hospital. Sit here. I'll be right back." She ran to the truck, found the keys, and tore across the field to where she'd left Maggie. It took some maneuvering, but she managed to get Maggie into the back seat of the crew cab. A towel on the seat appeared mostly clean, so she wrapped it around Maggie's leg, then jumped into the driver's seat to find Kate already ensconced in the front passenger seat. "I'd tell you to stay here, but I don't have time to argue," she said, driving out of the field.

"Put your horse in the barn." Maggie's voice was faint, but strong enough to penetrate Tobie's controlled panic.

"No time."

"Not safe in that small trailer." She glanced in the rearview mirror and saw Maggie attempting to sit up.

"Stubborn damn woman," Tobie said. She pulled out her phone. "Siri, call Ricky." Thank God she still had his number in her phone.

"Hey, Ms. Mason. You find your horse?"

"No, not yet. But I'm at your aunt's house. She's been hurt pretty bad. I need directions to the nearest hospital."

"Crap. I was just pulling up at the sheriff's office to begin my shift. If you're still at her ranch, take a right out of the driveway. When you reach the second stoplight in town, hang a left, and it's about a half mile down that road. You're only five minutes or so away. I'll meet you there."

Tobie gunned the truck and skidded out onto the highway. Three minutes later, she parked outside a building that wasn't exactly a hospital but a full-service emergency room. Ricky was standing outside his patrol car, waiting for them.

"Her leg is cut pretty bad," she told him as he helped her get Maggie out of the truck.

"Get your horse in the barn. Not safe." Maggie grabbed Ricky's arm. "Make her go put that horse in the barn. Tornadoes coming."

"I will, Aunt Maggie. I'll go do it myself. I'll get your animals in the barn, too." He looked up at Tobie. "That is, if you'll stay with her."

"Sure. I'll stay." She handed him the keys to her truck. All she could think about was Maggie. Had she lost too much blood?

"Well, well, well." A huge guy in scrubs and a nametag identifying him as a nurse arrived with a wheelchair. "You just can't stay out of trouble, can you, Ms. Maggie?"

Maggie gave him a weak smile. "I was missing all of you, so I split my leg open with the disc harrow." She was chalk white, so Tobie was shocked that she could still joke.

They were about to go inside when Tobie stopped. "Kate's in Maggie's truck," she said to Ricky.

He waved for them to continue inside. "I'll need her to help me get the goats and chickens in the barn, so I'll take her with me."

"Anything changed since your last ER visit?" the nurse asked as he rolled Maggie into the emergency room.

"No," she said, closing her eyes and wincing as they bumped over the channels for the automatic doors.

"She's lost a lot of blood," Tobie said, trotting alongside them. "I don't know how long that tourniquet has been on her leg. She was unconscious when I found her, so she didn't know either. I released it, but blood started to spurt, so I had to immediately retighten it."

Nurses and doctors appeared from nowhere and collectively lifted her onto a bed as a male doctor began to issue orders. A nurse helped Maggie out of her shirt, then grabbed her arm to start an IV saline drip, while another began attaching monitors to her chest and hand, and still another cut the leg of her jeans away from the injured calf.

Maggie protested weakly. "Stop, stop. These are my favorite jeans."

"Well, they're going to be your favorite shorts now," the nurse said.

"Does she have any drug allergies?" the doctor asked Tobie.

A chorus of "no" came from the nurses.

"Ah. I see the staff knows you here."

"Where's Dr. Berger?" Maggie asked as the nurse inserted a dose of morphine into her IV.

"She's out on pregnancy leave."

"Had a little girl last week," one of the nurses said.

"That's nice," Maggie said, her pupils widening as the drug kicked in.

"I'm Doctor Oh, filling in here for a few months until she returns," the doctor said.

"Oh. Doctor Oh, Doc-O. Ee-i-ee-i-Oh." Maggie's clumsy singing of the old children's song dissolved into a mumble as her eyes drooped.

"You are one lucky lady," Dr. Oh said. "You cut into the muscle and nicked an artery, but missed any bone or tendons. You'll need a lot of stitches, but we don't have to transfer you to a hospital. I can do this here. We're going to have to get these jeans off because I'm going to cast that leg after I stitch it up to immobilize that muscle until it can knit back together."

Maggie's eyes popped open, but her voice was slurred. "Don't cut my jeans."

"That's what you're going to bitch about," the male nurse said, chuckling. "I guess you didn't hear the cast part."

Adrenaline, the banter between the nurses who seemed to know Maggie well, and the fast pace of the team working on her had distracted Tobie. But when the doctor began irrigating the gaping wound, her stomach did a little flip-flop, and she leaned against the wall.

"Uh-oh." The male nurse grabbed Tobie's arm. "If you're thinking of throwing up or passing out, I vote for passing out." He guided her out of the treatment room and into a waiting room with about six other people. "You sit right here, and I'll get you a soda." He disappeared for a minute and returned with a can of Coca-Cola.

"I usually just drink water or coffee," she said.

"Trust me. You're coming down from a big adrenaline rush, and the sugar and carbonation in this drink will make you feel a lot better. I'll come back later and let you know how she's doing, and the doc will give you her discharge orders when he's done so you can take her home." He started to leave her, then stopped. "It's going to be a while, so you might want to take a break and come back in an hour or two. If you don't want to leave, there's a general store across the street where you can probably find some sweatpants, because she won't be able to get those jeans back on over the cast."

"Good idea. Thanks."

Chapter Twelve

The nurse turned up the level of light in the treatment room, rousing the dozing patient.

"Look. It's brown-eyes. She's bringing me some pants. Can't leave without pants."

The nurse patted Maggie's hand. "That's right. Now let's get those pants on so you can go home."

Tobie stood at the end of Maggie's bed, a little shocked at her greeting. When the nurse held out her hand, she recovered. "Oh, right." She handed over the generic gray sweatpants she'd picked up at the store across the street after she'd switched Maggie's truck for her own and moved her rig from the campground into Maggie's equipment barn.

"Help me get these on over her cast," the nurse said. "The cut was deep, and we pretty much had to knock her out to stitch that muscle back together. She'll be semi-awake for a while but should sleep it off once you get her home."

"Damn rock jumped out of the ground and attacked my harrow. Then it attacked me. Nearly chewed my leg off." Maggie drunkenly sat up and knocked her knuckles against the fiberglass cast.

Tobie raised her eyebrows, surprised. "That's more than I've ever heard her say…unless she's talking about horses," she told the nurse.

"Yep. Morphine knocks most people out, but it turns her into a regular motormouth. She won't remember much about what she's saying now, so if you have anything you want to ask her, the ride home is the time to do it. The stuff we sedated her with is as good as truth serum."

"I don't—" She'd almost admitted she didn't know Maggie that well but stopped herself. This could be fun. "That's good to know," she said, nodding.

Maggie was wearing black cotton hip-hugging underwear that were basically modest, but Tobie still tried to divert her eyes. One glance at those long, muscular legs—well, leg, because one was in a cast above the knee—and defined abdomen made Tobie's insides clench in a good—but inappropriate in this situation—way.

"There you go," the nurse said. "Let's sit up, and you move your butt to the edge of the bed so your friend and I can help you into this wheelchair."

"No wheelchair. They gave me crutches," Maggie said, pointing to the metal ones leaning in the corner of the room.

The nurse ignored her, pulling Maggie's right arm over her shoulder, so Tobie did the same on the other side. "You're way too groggy to manage those crutches."

"Am not." Maggie attempted to stand but swayed and fell back to sit on the bed again.

"Do you want to go home?" the nurse asked.

"Yes." Maggie jutted her chin and lower lip out like a six-year-old about to throw a tantrum. "Give me my crutches."

"I want you to go home, too. You've been the most difficult patient I've had this week. But the only way you're getting out of here is in that wheelchair. It's up to you."

"Fine."

Maggie let them help her stand, but because of Tobie's six-foot height, she leaned more heavily on her than the nurse. She looked up at Tobie. "You're taller than me." Her eyes were impossibly blue, because the drugs they had given her delayed her pupils from responding to the level of light in the room.

"Yup," Tobie said, smiling at Maggie's slurred words. "Six feet and a few inches. You're pretty tall, too."

"Ow." Maggie winced when she tried to put her weight on her casted foot. "I can't walk with this thing on my leg."

"You're not supposed to walk or put weight on that leg at all," the nurse said. "If you do, you'll pull your stitches out."

Maggie looked up at Tobie. "I've gotten myself in a stitch." Then she laughed loudly.

Tobie had to laugh, too, because this funny version of the very intense Maggie Wilkes was so unexpected. "I'm not sure that's the right word you're looking for, but you certainly are a stitch when you're drugged up."

"I'm a stitch?"

Tobie chuckled. "You have me in stitches."

Maggie's eyes widened. "Oh, no. You got hurt, too?"

"No. You got hurt. I'm fine."

They arrived at Tobie's truck, but she realized getting Maggie up into the back seat was going to be a challenge.

"Let me go get some help," the nurse said. She returned promptly with Maggie's crutches and the big male nurse who'd originally helped them inside.

Tobie climbed into the back seat and hooked her arms under Maggie's to pull her inside, while the two nurses grabbed her legs and hoisted her up into the crew cab.

The big nurse patted Maggie's uninjured leg. "Try to stay out of trouble for a while, Ms. Maggie." Having succumbed to the drugs again, she answered with a quiet snore. He smiled and shook his head. "You're going to need help getting her in the house," he said as he put the crutches in the bed of the truck.

"Her nephew, Ricky, is at the house and can call more help if we need it." Tobie gave up trying to figure out a way to belt her in and hoped that, if she drove slowly, Maggie wouldn't get tossed onto the floor of the truck.

The female nurse handed Tobie a sheet of discharge instructions. "The doctor wants you to bring her back in ten days to cut that cast off and remove the stitches."

"Okay."

"And the doctor called in pain meds and an antibiotic she'll need to start tonight. They should be ready by now." She pointed to the parking lot exit. "The pharmacy is about two blocks to the left." She put a hand on the truck. "Take good care of her. She's a special lady. She tends to a lot more than wild horses around here."

"Thanks. I will," Tobie said. It seemed unnecessary to explain she didn't plan to be around very long.

❖

The wind had grown stronger, so strong she could feel the crosswinds trying to push her heavy-duty truck off the road while she picked up Maggie's medicine and returned to her farm. Ricky's cruiser was parked next to the house, but he was nowhere in sight, so she sounded the truck's horn a few times because she needed his help to get their patient inside. He appeared instantly, jogging toward her from the barn when the first spatters of rain hit.

"Let's get her in the house before this shower turns into a downpour," she said, opening the door behind Maggie and climbing inside. "See if you can grab that cast above the knee, and her other leg. I'll try to slide her your way. Gently, though." She sat Maggie upright, then wrapped her arms around her chest to lift her slightly. She was dead weight. "Maggie, I need you to wake up and help us get you inside." The only answer she got was a snore-snort.

"Man, she's really out. What'd they give her?" Ricky asked. He was strong for his very average size but handled his aunt gently and with great care.

"Be glad she's sleeping. She was a regular chatterbox before we got her in the truck and she passed out again."

He laughed. "I would have loved to hear that."

"The nurse said the sedation sometimes affects people like a truth serum. Got anything you want to ask her? They said she probably wouldn't remember it tomorrow."

"I'll think on that. Right now, we need to figure out how to get her in the house."

They managed to move her to the edge of the bench seat's end but weren't sure what to do from there. Tobie backed out of the truck and came around to stand next to Ricky. Maggie's feet were dangling out of the truck, and he was struggling to hold her weight while she slumped toward him.

Maggie was slender but large-boned and muscled from farm work. Tobie figured she weighed at least one-fifty or one-sixty.

"We could do a two-person seat carry, but she's not awake enough to hold on to us. We'd probably end up dropping her." She wanted to study the situation, but the occasional big drops of rain were becoming more frequent. "Let me have her."

She maneuvered over to take Maggie's weight, then turned and used Maggie's arms to pull her onto her back in a backpack-style carry. She leaned forward, and Maggie's head fell forward on her shoulder.

"You're kind of cute." Maggie's words were soft and still slurred, but they made Tobie smile and her knees go weak.

"You might not think so in a few minutes if I drop you because you're sweet-talking in my ear."

"Okay." Warm breath from a deep sigh brushed Tobie's neck, sending goosebumps down her arm.

Tobie steeled herself and got a good grip on Maggie's arms. "Here we go." Her taller height left Maggie's legs dangling. "Hurry up and get the door. She's pretty heavy."

Ricky ran ahead, and Tobie thanked the stars there were three easy steps onto the porch.

"Put her down in the recliner," he said. "She sleeps there some nights when her back is bothering her."

The old farmhouse had been renovated inside into an open concept so that the kitchen, dining, and living area were one large room with a clear path to the indicated chair. The lounger was grouped with a leather couch and a couple of end tables that faced a large-screen television. A wood stove sat in the corner on a stone hearth, and a large, faded, braided rug held it all together. Cozy.

Ricky held onto the casted leg while Tobie squatted to lower Maggie, and then he pressed the buttons on the side of the chair to recline it and raise the footrest to support her legs. He very sweetly took his aunt's hand in his when her eyes opened and focused on him. "Aunt Maggie, that storm is rolling in, but I've got everybody safe and fed in the barn. I'm going to put Kate's bed next to your chair, but I have to go back to work now. Do you want me to call Mom to come stay with you?"

This question apparently cut through the drug haze, and her eyes widened. "Oh, hell, no." Her words were still slurred but loud. She closed her eyes and quieted, but continued to mumble. "She might be my sister, but I'm not listening to that damned woman preach to me about going to church and finding some man to marry. I don't need anybody to take care of me. I do fine all by myself."

He squeezed her hand. "How about Tobie staying with you tonight?"

She didn't open her eyes, but she smiled. "Brown-eyes? Is she coming over?"

Tobie's face heated, but she squeezed Maggie's shoulder. "I'm here now, Maggie. I just brought you home from the hospital."

"You'd still be lying out there in the dirt if she hadn't found you. She took you to the emergency room. Brice closed the campground and hightailed it to Florida because of the storm, so we put her horse in your barn and her trailers in the equipment shed."

"Okay."

"You'll let her stay with you?" he asked.

Her smile turned into a frown. "Don't need anybody to stay with me."

Tobie shook her head. "I need a place to stay, and you could use a little help for a few days, so it works out for both of us."

Eyes still closed, Maggie smiled, her words fading to a near whisper. "Okay then."

Ricky went down the hallway and returned with several pillows and two blankets. He tucked a pillow under his aunt's leg and covered her with one of the blankets. "I really appreciate your help with her." He pointed to the kitchen. "Feel free to plunder the pantry for something to eat. She normally keeps it stocked. It's the fresh stuff she runs out of because she hates grocery shopping, but I checked out the refrigerator, and it looks like she went to the store recently. The milk and orange juice are fresh."

"You seem close to your aunt."

"I love my mother, and Aunt Maggie does, too. But Mom is a lot to deal with, so I used to come stay with Aunt Maggie for weeks in the summer when I was a kid, and pretty much lived here half of my teen years."

"She's lucky to have you to look out for her." Since Tobie's grandmother died, she had no family close to her.

"I'm lucky to have her."

Maggie snuggled under the blanket and muttered something unintelligible.

Ricky grinned. "They said she wouldn't remember much until she sleeps this off?"

Tobie eyed him suspiciously. "The nurse said she *probably* wouldn't remember *much*."

He knelt next to his aunt. "Aunt Maggie, don't you think Tobie's pretty?"

"Brown-eyes," she mumbled without opening her eyes. "Handsome woman."

"Good-looking enough that you want to kiss her?"

Maggie licked her lips, but her answer was a long snore. She was out again.

"You better hope she doesn't remember this, or she'll have your ass as soon as she can chase you down."

He laughed quietly and gave his sleeping aunt a long look. "They give you prescriptions for her?"

"They called them in, and I picked up her medicine from the pharmacy on the way home. It's on the front seat of the truck, along with a sheet of discharge instructions."

"I'll go get it and her crutches." He indicated the extra pillow and blanket he'd laid on the couch. "I don't know how long it's been since she had a guest, so that extra bedroom is probably dusty as hell."

"I can always go sleep in my camper, but the couch will be fine tonight. I probably need to stay close until she's able to get around on the crutches."

He nodded and left to retrieve the medicine and crutches. When he returned, he'd also gone to his patrol car and picked up a long raincoat and a cover for his hat. He stood by the door because he was dripping wet and held out the items for her. "I see that the instructions say for her to ice that leg to keep it from swelling inside the cast. She keeps three or four ice packs in the freezer for when her back acts up. Also, there's wood on the porch for the stove over there if this storm brings in a cold front, and some camping lanterns and flashlights in the closet by the front door in case you lose power tonight."

The radio on his belt squawked a second of static before the dispatcher spoke. "Ricky, you got your aunt settled yet?"

He keyed the mike attached to his shoulder. "Roger that."

"We need you over at the diner. The wind has uprooted one of those big pines, and it took out two cars and the power line."

"Be there in five." He paused at the door. "When she has her senses back, don't let her bully you into leaving. She'll try, and if she gets to be too much of a pain, just threaten to call my mom. It works every time." He waved his good-bye and left.

The house felt blissfully quiet after the chaos of the accident and scrambling to secure everything before the storm hit. After giving Maggie's cast a good sniff and her hand a lick, Kate curled up in the bed Ricky had placed next to the recliner. Rain drummed against the house's metal roof in a steady, soothing white noise.

Tobie retrieved two ice packs from the freezer and laid them gently on the bottom half of the cast. Then she tucked the soft sherpa blanket around Maggie's shoulders and whispered, "I think you're a handsome woman, too, blue-eyes."

CHAPTER THIRTEEN

Tobie woke to loud crashes and the sound of wood splintering. She jumped to her feet and ran to the front door. The sky had taken on an eerie gray cast so she could see the tree limbs and debris twirling and twisting into the sky. A tornado appeared to be moving through the heavily wooded property across the road from Maggie's long driveway. Tobie slammed the door shut and set the deadbolt, then rushed over to Maggie's chair.

"Maggie, Maggie. Wake up for me, sweetie. Do you have a basement?"

"What? No." She tried to sit up and groaned. "Fuck, that hurts."

"A tornado's coming." Tobie couldn't stop her voice from rising. "We're too exposed here."

"Storm cellar's outside." Maggie rubbed her eyes, which widened when she turned her head to the floor-length windows on the front of the house. "Too late for that. Kate, pantry. Go hide."

Kate whirled in a circle, jumped against Maggie's chair, then ran into the kitchen's pantry at Maggie's continued urging.

Tobie turned in time to see the twister tearing through the woods, moving in a path parallel to the road. But tornadoes had a dangerous habit of zigzagging or hopping to new points of destruction, and Tobie didn't intend to take a chance it would stay on its path and miss them. She grabbed her quilt from the couch and flung herself on top of Maggie, cast be damned. Her quilt covered them both from head to toe, and she slid her hands between the recliner's arms and seat to grab hold of the chair's iron frame. If the tornado sucked them up, it'd have to take the chair, too.

The seconds that followed seemed like hours. Tobie closed her eyes tight and prayed, even though she wasn't a religious person. She turned her head away and pressed her forehead against Maggie's temple when something hit the front windows. The quilt, she knew, didn't offer much protection, but she hoped it would hold off most of the glass shards. She was scared. This was the closest she'd ever come to dying, and all she could think about was her desire, her need to kiss Maggie. So, she did.

❖

Maggie's leg hurt like a son of a bitch, but Tobie's leg wedged against her crotch felt surprisingly good. Then before her brain was able to figure out the conflicting feelings—I hurt, I feel good— warm lips were on hers, and a hot tongue was asking entrance into her mouth. She responded without hesitating.

Tobie's lips were slightly chapped, probably from being outdoors so much in her hunt for Sarah's Heart, but her mouth was silk. For fuck's sake, she'd forgotten the exhilaration of kissing another woman, and she barely heard the glass shattering next to her and pelting the blanket that covered them.

The clattering of glass stopped. All noise stopped. And Tobie went still.

They both drew back as much as their position, cramped together in the lounger, allowed. Frozen, they listened to the silence.

Tobie threw off the quilt and carefully extracted herself from the recliner. Maggie watched her, but Tobie avoided her gaze.

Maggie let the uncomfortable silence hang in the air for several minutes before Tobie began to fidget.

"Sorry," Tobie said. "I'm sorry. I guess the danger and adrenaline got the best of me. I thought I might be breathing my last if that tornado hit the house."

Maggie watched her shake glass out of the quilt that had covered them and fold it, then push the five-foot limb sticking through the window out onto the porch. "I should board this up until you can get it fixed."

"So, I guess you wouldn't have kissed me if you hadn't thought you were going to die in the next few minutes?"

"No. Yes." Tobie dug her toe into the worn rug and shrugged her shoulder to rub it against her cheek. "I mean, I've wanted to kiss you before now. I just didn't think you wanted to kiss me."

Maggie laughed. "You're shy? I figured that, with your looks, you've probably had women jumping into your truck if you even slowed down when you drove through a town."

Tobie scoffed. "As if." She kicked at the rug and shrugged again. "I've been too busy, working and settling my grandmother's affairs after she died." She cleared her throat, and when she finally looked up, Maggie fell into those soft brown eyes and suddenly found herself feeling a little shy, too. "Besides. I'm not really a one-night-stand kind of girl," Tobie said. "I mean, I have, but only a few times, and I wasn't comfortable with it."

Maggie was the one who looked away this time. "Me, too. And me, neither." She cleared her throat. "There's some wood in the barn you could use to board up that window."

"Okay." Tobie seemed relieved to move back to safer ground. "Where's your broom? I need to sweep up this glass before Kate cuts her foot on it."

"It's in the walk-in pantry in the kitchen. You can tell Kate to come out now." She shifted in the chair. She was uncomfortable asking Tobie for help, but, damn, she was hurting. "I need to pee. Can you help me up and hand me those crutches?"

"Can you manage the crutches now? If you fall, you could tear out those stitches."

"I've had crutches before. I know how to use them."

She threw her blanket aside, lowered the footrest, and scooted to the front of the chair in preparation while Tobie fetched the crutches.

"Wait a second while I clear away up some of this glass." Tobie swept the glass into a corner, then handed over the crutches. "No weight on that foot, the doc said."

Maggie's insides clenched—in a good way—when Tobie pressed against her side to shoulder under one of her arms to help her stand. "Thanks. I can handle it from here."

"I'm going to walk behind you, just to make sure you don't get dizzy," Tobie said.

When they reached the door to the small hallway bathroom,

Maggie maneuvered past the sink to the toilet. Tobie started to follow her inside, but Maggie put a hand on Tobie's chest and gave a gentle push. "I've got it, okay? This isn't my first rodeo with a casted leg." She pointed to a thick bar where a towel hung adjacent to the walk-in shower. "That's not a towel bar. It's a pull-up bar installed when I broke my other leg several years ago. I'll yell if I need any help."

Tobie obediently backed out of the bathroom and pulled the door closed. "I'll be out here sweeping up the glass," she said from the other side of the door.

When Maggie emerged from the bathroom and settled in her chair again, the drugs had definitely worn off, and her leg was throbbing like a drum. Tobie had finished cleaning up the glass.

"Should I feed Kate?" she asked.

"Her food's in the pantry. Scoop's in the bag, and she gets one full measure in her bowl." Maggie pointed to the dog bowls in the kitchen. "But before you do that, I think I need a pain pill and two new ice packs."

"No problem." Tobie brought over Maggie's medicines and a bottle of water. "One of these is in case the pain pills make you nauseous. The other is an antibiotic. But you need to eat something first."

"A sandwich will be fine. There's some lunch meat in the bottom drawer of the refrigerator. Make yourself one, too. And could you find my phone?"

Tobie produced Maggie's phone from her own pocket. "Got it right here." She handed it over and returned to the kitchen, where Maggie heard her feed Kate and make sandwiches. She was chewing hers when she brought Maggie's over to her.

"Thanks." Maggie took the sandwich, but Tobie was still avoiding her stare. She watched Tobie head to the back door, the other half of her sandwich in her hand. The air between them felt awkward. She called to Tobie when she opened the door. The rain had slowed to a fine drizzle. "Hey, brown-eyes."

Tobie smiled when she turned and, at last, held Maggie's gaze.

Heat crawled up her neck, but she softened her voice. "I've wanted to kiss you, too…before."

Tobie's smile was blazing, but she only nodded and headed for the barn.

"Shit," Maggie said to Kate after the door closed behind Tobie. "Why did I admit that? It's either the drugs or I've lost my ever-loving mind."

Kate gave Maggie a side-eye and wagged her tail.

CHAPTER FOURTEEN

So, where's brown-eyes?" Cindy bustled around the kitchen, making Maggie's favorite pecan waffles and bacon, even though it was lunchtime, well past breakfast.

"What?" Maggie nearly spit her coffee across the room. She glared at Cindy. "That fucking nosy nurse. I'm going to sue her for a HIPAA violation."

Cindy laughed. "Don't glare at me. I became immune to that years ago. Carrie only told me because she knows we have a history and are probably each other's best friend now. Besides, she didn't violate any HIPAA laws. She'd have to give out your medical information, so you can't sue her."

Maggie shifted uncomfortably in her chair. "Tobie's out checking my fences and trail cameras."

The morning had dawned clear and bright on the damage caused by the tornado. The pine forest on the other side of the road had suffered a twenty-foot swath of trees uprooted and turned into kindling. Fortunately, her farm—as much as she could tell from the house—had been spared. Tobie had mounted up early, taking a map of Maggie's farm and trail cameras to check that nothing else was damaged. The sorghum fields were mostly turned under, but she wanted to make sure the fences were intact so the horses couldn't get in and graze on that last half acre of fodder, which was toxic to them. Also, several of the cameras had gone dark, but Maggie gave her a bag of extras if some needed to be replaced. She could probably repair any damaged ones, especially since she couldn't do much until the cast was removed and her stitches came out.

"Who's that out on your tractor?"

"Ricky. He's finishing that field for me. I was two-thirds done when a stone got stuck in the harrow and I cut my leg trying to get it out."

"Is that the only field? I can send Jake over on Saturday if you have more that need turning under." Jake was Cindy's husband and father to her three kids. Even though she and Cindy had once been lovers, Maggie genuinely liked Jake.

"That field is the last, but thanks for offering."

"Come over here to the table to eat. If I serve you in that chair, you'll have syrup everywhere." Cindy set two plates of steaming waffles on the table, then came over to take Maggie's coffee cup to refill. "Need some help getting up?"

"No. They must have poured twenty IV bags in me yesterday, so I had to get up to pee a million times last night. I got lots of practice on the crutches."

Cindy brought over the syrup she'd been warming in the microwave, along with a couple of pills. "Brown-eyes said you needed to take these with your lunch."

"Her name is Tobie." Maggie's glare was ignored again. "And I don't need the one for nausea."

"She said you would say that. I think she's got your number already. Smart woman." She pushed the pills closer to Maggie. "Take them all."

"The nausea pill makes me sleepy."

"Good. You need to rest. I know you. As soon as I leave, you're going to try to crutch yourself out to the barn to check everything. Ricky's already done that, milked and fed everybody. He showed Tobie the ropes so she can feed tonight while he's working. I'll send Jake over, too, to make sure she's mastered the milking part. So quit whining and swallow those pills."

"You're still bossy as ever."

"How else could I manage a husband and three wild children, plus run a business?"

Maggie swallowed the pills with some coffee, then crammed a big bite of waffle in her mouth and hummed. "So good," she said around the mouthful.

Cindy smiled and shook her head at Maggie's occasional bad table manners. They'd met through friends as juniors in college. Cindy majored in business, while Maggie took agriculture classes. They'd dated for two years, then roomed together through grad school. After they graduated, however, they took different paths.

Maggie had been constantly at odds with her father after her mother died of cancer before Maggie left for college. She came home with a doctorate in environmental science and a backpack full of organic farming ideas that her father rejected. Her resentment and rebellion manifested in her coming out and proud in their small town.

Cindy wasn't that brave and turned out to be truly bisexual. She got a loan to buy the restaurant, then aptly named it Cindy's Diner. Others had tried opening eating places, but none survived when trying to compete with hers. She was a decent chef but preferred to be out front, chatting with everyone who came in. So, she hired a cook and taught him how to make some of her signature dishes, even though she didn't let anyone else prepare her popular beef stew. Her menu contained a mixture of traditional country cooking and a few fancy dishes like omelets and gumbo. She liked to joke that she'd married Jake, who was from Louisiana, for his gumbo recipe.

Cindy caught her up on the latest town gossip while they ate, then cleaned up their dishes while Maggie settled back into her chair. She was growing sleepy from her full stomach and the medicine. She dozed off but woke when Cindy placed fresh ice packs on her leg and kissed her cheek. Although their sexual relationship was in the distant past, they still held a deep affection for each other.

"I'm going now, sweetie. I've left chicken and dumplings in the fridge for supper."

"No gumbo? You always cook gumbo on Wednesdays." She rubbed her eyes, trying to wake up more. "I love your gumbo."

"Yes, and the spices always upset your stomach."

"I prefer to think of it as a cleanse."

Cindy chuckled and shook her head. "Do you really want a case of diarrhea when you can't hop up and run to the bathroom?"

Maggie smiled, too, and shook her head. "Good point. Chicken and dumplings sounds great. Thanks, Cinders."

Cindy smiled at the old nickname and bent to kiss her cheek again. "Don't give Tobie a hard time. If I wasn't married with three kids and stretch marks, I might try to lose a few pounds and jump on that hottie myself."

Maggie turned away, pretending to look out the windows until she realized she'd forgotten they were boarded up. "I kissed her."

Cindy straightened. "What? You kissed her? You're just bringing this up now, when I have to leave?"

"Yeah. I wasn't sure I wanted to tell anyone." She turned back to Cindy. "I haven't wanted to kiss someone in a very long time."

"Did she kiss you back?"

"Actually, she kissed me, and I kissed her back."

Cindy squatted next to her and held her gaze. "Oh, honey. I didn't know you were interested. I won't tease you about her anymore."

"I'm eight years older than she is."

"That doesn't matter once you both clear the thirty-year mark. Besides, she seems very mature for her early thirties. She's built her own business, and I'm qualified to tell you that isn't at all easy."

"She's only here until she catches her horse that got away."

"Unless you give her a reason to stay. I know she hauls horses for a living, but she has to have a home base somewhere."

Maggie frowned at the old cliché of lesbians moving in together after the second date. Wait. Tobie didn't need a U-Haul to move in. All her belongings were already in that huge horse camper-trailer parked in the equipment shed. That realization made Maggie a little uneasy and at the same time pleased, since it meant Tobie would at least be around for supper. "We kissed. I didn't ask her to move in."

"Just take it one step at a time. You don't show it much, but I know you have a romantic, sentimental side. Give her a chance to see it."

A mixture of fear and longing filled her. "I don't know."

"Just think about it after you take a nap." Cindy patted her arm and stood. "I'll send Jake over about six o'clock to help milk."

"Okay." Her eyelids were growing heavy. "Take a tub of cheese from the goat-barn cooler for the diner." She closed her eyes, and Cindy's good-bye was the last thing she heard before the drugs carried her into a deep sleep.

❖

Muddy was favoring his left front foot a little, and Tobie found a small, sharp stone wedged between his hoof and metal shoe. He seemed fine after she dug it out with a hoof pick, but she decided to saddle Maggie's mule instead. After all, she'd be checking Maggie's fences and cameras for her.

Her saddlebags were stuffed with extra cameras, if any needed replacing, a sandwich, and a halter and lead in case she was able to catch Heart. She was getting started later than she wanted, but they'd spent a restless evening and night, with Maggie waking every three to four hours to pee, swap out her ice packs, and take more pain medicine. Consequently, they'd slept until nearly seven o'clock, and then she had to cook breakfast for them both. Cindy called to say she'd bring lunch for their patient, so before heading to the barn, Tobie had tucked Maggie into the lounger with a bottle of water and the television remote within reach.

Neither spoke about *the kiss*, but the weight of it hung in the air like another approaching storm. On the other hand, last night's storm had given way to sunny skies and a freshly washed landscape. It also left a trail of destruction—uprooted trees, muddy pastures, and swollen creeks.

She followed the fence line Maggie had marked on a map for her, stopping in only one place to hammer a board back into place. Other than puddles yet to soak into the ground, she saw few trees close enough to fall across the fences. The ones that were nearby had either weathered the storm or fallen in a different direction. She was glad, because she was eager to patrol the trails for a glimpse of Heart.

Maggie had helped her download an app that showed the camera feeds on her phone. She flipped through the views and compared them to Maggie's map to find the nearest one that wasn't working, then pointed Penny toward it.

She learned during their fence patrol that the mule determined her own pace, pinning her ears back but going no faster than a trot no matter how hard Tobie dug her heels into her sides or slapped her butt with the end of the reins. But when they turned to cross the unfenced hay fields and ride the wildlife trails, Penny broke into a smooth canter, ears forward and nostrils flaring to pick up the woodland scents.

Tobie had replaced two cameras and remounted a third when the forest opened up to a wide plain of wet desert sand. She expected the cacti but was surprised by the wildflowers that dotted the landscape of red dirt, an occasional scrubby bush, and tough grasses. Two herds, a good distance apart, were grazing on the flowers and stripping bushes of any greenery. The stallions appeared wary of each other and steered any of their group away if they wandered too near the other herd. She smiled. One stallion was the dark stud, and Heart was grazing at his side.

Tobie moved uphill and used her binoculars to get a closer look. Heart moved stiffly and occasionally twisted around to nudge her belly. Was she suffering from colic? It was possible, since she wasn't used to eating the roughage that horses lived on in the wild. She sucked in a breath. It was difficult to tell on Heart's dark brown coat, but she appeared to have a bloody wound on her belly, near her hind legs.

She dismounted and tied Penny to a flimsy bush. The mule might not stray from Maggie, but she didn't trust that Penny wouldn't suddenly decide to head home and leave her to walk. She retrieved Heart's halter and lead from her saddle bags, as well as a bunch of carrots—leafy tops still intact—that she'd found in Maggie's pantry.

Tobie walked carefully closer to Night's group, stopping when several of the horses raised their heads and stared at her. She didn't want to send them running. Then she put her fingers to her mouth and let out a low whistle like she'd seen Sarah do in the video she'd watched. Heart's head came up instantly, her ears flicking back and forth. When Tobie whistled again and held up the carrots, the mare began to move toward her.

The stallion watched and followed about halfway but didn't interfere since she wasn't moving toward the other stallion's group. The mare walked directly to her but sniffed her over thoroughly before snatching the carrots from her. Heart didn't pull away when Tobie carefully looped the lead line around her neck and even lowered her head for the halter while she chewed the last of the carrots. Her wound didn't look deep, but was a long gash from mid-belly to her teats, where the flesh hung open. Black flies buzzed around it.

A walk back to the farm would take a long time, so she thought a moment, then thumbed Ricky's contact on her cell phone.

"Hey, it's Tobie Mason. I got my mare, but she's injured. Can you go to Maggie's and bring the two-horse trailer to pick us up?"

"Sure." His answer was immediate. "Send me your GPS coordinates, and I'll see how close I can get to your location. Then I'll send you the coordinates for where we can meet up."

"Thanks, man. I really appreciate all your help."

"No problem. I'm on duty, but this shift has been quieter than a church. I'm happy to have something to do."

❖

Tobie exhaled a relieved breath when she saw Maggie's truck and the smaller trailer waiting on the logging road. It had been a slow, tense walk, with Heart grunting in pain occasionally. Ricky had already turned the truck around for a return trip to the farm and waved when she got closer. He whistled long and low when he looked at the gash in Heart's belly.

"Good thing you found her. With a wound like this, coyotes and maybe a mountain lion would sniff her out right away."

"I know. Maggie would write it off as the circle of life, but I'm not going to leave this injured mare to be eaten by anyone."

Ricky removed Penny's saddle and substituted a halter for her bridle, tossing the tack into the truck's bed. "Don't misjudge my aunt. I've seen her grieve for weeks when something happens to one of her wild ones. But she believes, like the Native Americans that were here before white men, that the wild horses came before the cattle and shouldn't be penned and subjected to forced domestication or end up in a Mexican slaughterhouse."

Tobie climbed into the truck after they loaded the horses, and Ricky slid into the driver's seat since it was his aunt's truck. "That's a mouthful. Are you her public-relations guy or something?"

He grinned. "I might look like a small-town deputy, but Aunt Maggie made sure I got a college education."

"What was your major?"

"Computer technology and web design. I'm a field deputy and the town's IT department all in one. I designed the town's website and Aunt Maggie's, too. Our town isn't big enough for a full-time IT person, and I enjoy being out in the field, so it's a win-win for me and the town."

"Are you going to be sheriff one day?"

"Don't want to be sheriff. Me and Cathy, my fiancée, are getting married in a few months, and we want to start a family. I don't intend to be one of those guys who's working so much they don't have time to spend with their kids."

Tobie smiled. "Sounds like you're a man with a plan." She realized again that she really liked this guy. He was kind to his aunt, smart, and knew what he wanted in life. She'd always thought she knew what she wanted—a unincumbered life traveling the country to haul horses. She'd never felt attached to a place, not even her grandmother's farm where she'd lived after her parents were killed. But this corner of Colorado, with its blue-eyed shield maiden guarding the wild horses, was growing on her.

Ricky's phone played the theme to the old 1960 *Bonanza* television show, and he put it on speaker. "Hey, Aunt Maggie."

"You pick 'em up yet?"

"Yeah. The mare has an ugly gash on her belly. Can you call Doc Vaughn to meet us at your place? She's going to need some stitches for sure."

"Everybody else okay?"

Tobie spoke up. "None of the other horses in her group appeared to be injured. She might have been panicked by the storm and went running through the woods, where a felled tree snagged her underside."

After a pause, Maggie said, "I'll call the doc. How far out are you?"

"ETA is about fifteen minutes," Ricky said.

"Okay. See you in fifteen."

The line went silent without so much as a good-bye, and Ricky chuckled. "I'm pretty sure she was asking about you, not the other horses," he said.

"Me? Why would she ask if I was okay?"

He shook his head. "I swear. I've never known two more clueless women in my life."

CHAPTER FIFTEEN

The vet was a sturdy woman with a sun-bleached ponytail and a skier's tan.

Tobie extended her hand. "Hi. I'm Tobie Mason—"

Before she could finish, the vet shook her hand quickly, then began handing her supplies to take into the barn. "I'm Mary Weston." She glanced up from the things she was gathering out of the cabinets in the back of her Chevrolet Tahoe. "You're that hauler that lost a Thoroughbred mare out on the highway."

"Yes. Please, call me Tobie." She led Dr. Weston into the wash stall, where Heart was cross-tied. "This is the horse. I probably caught up with her today only because she was apparently injured in that last storm."

Dr. Weston shook her head. "We've had freakish weather this year. I've treated more injuries than I care to count." She handed her stainless-steel bucket to Ricky, who filled it three-quarters full of warm water. The solar panels on the roof had warmed the barn and powered a tankless water heater. Dr. Weston sighed when she dipped her hands into the water and began scrubbing. "I love this barn. I think it's the only one in the county that has warm water." She looked around while she soaped her hands. "Where's Maggie?"

Tobie wanted to roll her eyes. "She sliced her leg up pretty good on the disc harrow, so she's in the house."

"I'm right here," Maggie said, hobbling in on her crutches. "How's it going, Doc?"

"Pretty good," Dr. Weston said, bending low to examine Heart's belly. "Is she pregnant?"

"No. She hasn't been bred," Tobie said, "unless that stallion she's taken up with got her. She's only been with him for about twelve days." She hurried to stack two bales of hay close by so Maggie could sit down without bending her injured leg.

"I could be wrong, but I'm seeing some signs that she's been in estrous. I'd need to ultrasound her to be sure."

"Vet exam and travel papers confirm she was a maiden mare when she left Kentucky."

"Then their vet must have missed something or falsified those papers. Who signed those travel papers?" Dr. Weston asked, placing her stethoscope at different spot on Heart's still relatively small belly.

"Dr. Stephen Benson," Tobie said.

Dr. Weston nodded. "I know him or, rather, know his reputation. He wouldn't miss something like this. If she is pregnant, she's carrying a mustang baby. It's late in the year for breeding, but being around a stallion probably triggered her to go into season."

"If she's pregnant, can we abort it?" Tobie asked.

"No!" Maggie used her crutch to push Tobie almost to the concrete floor of the wash stall. "If that's Night's baby, then it belongs to the Federal Bureau of Land Management. You are obligated to nurture this mare's pregnancy until birth. Once it's weaned, the baby will be released to join one of the wild herds, but the mare will be turned over to the insurance company that has already reimbursed the mare's buyer."

Dr. Weston turned to Ricky. "Can you get me a blanket that we can lay her down on? Those teats are very sensitive, and I think it's best if I knock her out, rather than use just a local."

Tobie's mind instantly jumped from Heart's future to her immediate crisis. She helped Ricky spread Penny's bad-weather blanket on the floor of the wash stall, and then they guided Heart down onto the blanket when her knees buckled from the sedation. Tobie wrapped a clean towel around her head to protect her eyes from any debris on the blanket.

With her lying on her side, they could assess the wound much easier. The tear in her gleaming coat began mid-belly and ended at her milk bag, which was impaled by at least a dozen long splinters.

"Damn. That's got to hurt," Ricky said.

Dr. Weston worked quickly, flushing the wound before she began removing the splinters. "I'll get all of these I can see, but we'll need to watch her closely for infection or other splinters abscessing to work their way out."

Ricky moved closer to aim his flashlight where Dr. Weston was working.

"Thanks. That extra light helps," Dr. Weston said.

"I found her like this today. I'm thinking that she got spooked in the storm and ran through the woods, where she tried to jump a downed tree but wasn't able to clear it," Tobie said.

"That makes sense, judging from the angle of the injury," Dr. Weston said.

"What are her chances of recovery?" Maggie asked.

"Have to wait and see. If we get lucky, and I can find most of these splinters, her chances are good. It's doubtful, though, that she'll recuperate enough to nurse a baby. These splinters have made a mess of her mammary equipment. The scar tissue will be extensive."

Ricky looked to Tobie. "Will the breeder still want her?"

Tobie shrugged. "Doubtful, unless they're willing to hand-raise any babies she has. Her bloodlines do trace back to Secretariat." The greatest horse in the history of racing had a reputation for passing his genes down through his daughters, who then gave birth to very fast colts. "But hand-raised babies don't generally make good racehorses. They're more interested in people than outrunning other horses."

"Can't they do invitro on horses? You know, take her fertilized eggs and implant them in another mare?" Ricky asked.

Tobie shook her head. "Not with racing Thoroughbreds. It has to be a live mating with witnesses." Her cell phone buzzed in her pocket, and she answered after checking the caller. "Hello? Yeah. This is Tobie Mason." She listened for a minute, looking at Maggie. "What? He said he'd give me two weeks to catch her, and I did that today. I've got his horse, and I'm only one day past the two weeks. Why did you pay the claim without checking with me?"

Her face darkened as she listened to the man on the other end of the call. "Yes. I'm having her checked by a vet right now. She's injured, but her prognosis is good. Dr. Mary Weston. Yes. I'll have her send you a report." She listened, then looked at her cell phone. The call had ended. "Shithead. He didn't even say good-bye. Just hung up."

"Insurance people don't like to pay out high-cost claims," Maggie said, shifting herself on the hay bales Tobie had brought over for her to sit on.

"What's the insurance company going to do with a retired racehorse?" Tobie was incredulous. "They can't do that."

"They can put her back on the track to win a few more purses, since that's all she might to be good for," Dr. Weston said. "If they keep racing her at her age, she'll end up breaking down."

"This horse has been retired from a lucrative racing career. She was headed to a California breeding farm," Tobie said.

"They could still get a baby out of her, but whether she could nurse it is the question," Dr. Weston said. "I'm not saying she won't be able to nurse a foal, but there's a chance she won't."

"Put that in your report," Maggie said. "All of it. And write a big, fat bill for her medical care."

Tobie was incredulous. "What? Then they'll try to race her for sure."

"Not if we offer to pay her vet bill and take her off their hands."

Tobie shook her head. "Her vet bill won't be a fraction of what they paid out for her, and everything I have is sunk into my rig. I can't afford to buy and keep a horse."

Maggie looked at Ricky, who was scratching his five o'clock stubble. "Ricky?"

He nodded. "I can come up with some ideas for raising the money."

"We're talking about tens of thousands of dollars." Tobie was a realist, not a save-the-wild horses idealist.

"Not for a six-year-old mare well past her racing age, because that will be how old she'll be by the time her foal is weaned," Maggie said.

"We don't know that she's pregnant," Tobie said.

"Mary?"

"Too early to confirm for sure. I can check her in a few more weeks." Dr. Weston plunked another long splinter into a stainless steel bowl. "That's the last one I can find," she said, holding out her hand for more stitching material. "It looks better than I thought, but we'll have to wait and see if I missed any. A few more stitches here and we can wake her up."

They watched in silence, each lost in their own thoughts, as Dr. Weston finished closing the gaping tear in Heart's milk bag.

"That should do it," Dr. Weston said, clutching her back as she rose from operating on her knees. Ricky offered his arm to help her stand. "Thanks, Ricky." Dr. Weston drew up another injection and pumped it into Heart's neck vein. "Tobie, Ricky, you guys get on her other side. She'll be wobbly when she stands. Don't push. Just brace her if she sways too much."

Heart began to struggle to her feet within minutes after the injection, and they steadied her until she appeared stable. Dr. Weston wrapped her torso in wide Ace bandages, with several sterile gauze pads.

"That should help keep that incision clean if she lies down. The wound will drain some, so you'll need to unwrap her, change the gauze pads daily, then rewrap her. But don't wrap too tight. It might cause swelling. I'll leave you more gauze, but you could use those pads they put on beds for human patients. They work especially well if she's out after a rain. But keep her in the stall for a week and walk her around several times during the day. That'll help keep the swelling down and keep her from getting too stiff. I'll be back next week unless you notice an abscess forming and want to call me sooner."

"That box stall on the right by the door is ready for her," Maggie said. "Jake came by to milk the goats while Ricky went out to meet you, and I had him lay fresh bedding in there."

Ricky helped Dr. Weston put her instruments away, while Tobie led the still-wobbly Heart into the stall. After drinking some water, the mare lowered her head and continued to sleep off the anesthesia while standing.

Tobie closed the stall door and pressed her forehead to the metal bars on the top half of the stall. She sighed but didn't turn around when Maggie crutched over and laid a warm hand on her shoulder.

"This is going to bankrupt my business right when I was taking it to the next level. The camper trailer is more than half paid for, but I still have payments to make. If I lose the rig, then I don't have a business. Hell, I don't have a home because I sold it to buy that fancy trailer."

"Worrying about that tonight won't fix anything," Maggie said, her voice soft. "We have options. Let's wait and see how she heals, and what Ricky can do for us."

Tobie shook her head. "What can Ricky do?" She turned to look at Maggie. "It's just business, and I shouldn't care, but I do. I don't want her sold at auction and maybe end up in a slaughterhouse because she's too old to race and can't have babies."

"Wait and see how she heals," Maggie said.

Overwhelmed, Tobie lurched forward and wrapped Maggie in a tight hug. After a moment's hesitation, Maggie hugged her back, pressing her cheek against Tobie's.

"We don't have to make any decisions tonight. Let's go inside and warm up some supper for us and Ricky."

❖

After consuming the chicken and dumplings Cindy had left them, Ricky set up an extra trail camera in Heart's stall so Tobie wouldn't go to the barn every thirty minutes to check on her. Then he headed home after giving his Aunt Maggie a sly grin and a kiss on the cheek. Yeah, Maggie knew he'd seen the hug in the barn. "I'm glad Tobie's here, so I won't worry about you being alone with your leg in a cast," he said.

Like the night before, Tobie helped Maggie bed down in her recliner. Maggie could see the worry in Tobie's eyes and caught Tobie's hand as she was fluffing the pillow under her leg for the tenth time. "Hey. She's going to be fine. Everything will be fine," she said.

Tobie's throat worked, and Maggie waited for her to choke down her emotion and speak. "I've just got so much on the line here, and I hurt for Heart. How do I know what's best for her? Do I throw away my livelihood for a horse? Is Sarah Carmichael looking down on us and wondering what the fuck we're doing with her Thoroughbred?"

Maggie tugged her down so that Tobie was kneeling next to her chair. She caressed her cheek and searched the deep well of those dark brown eyes. "I love that you care so much, but you've got to trust me that things will work out."

Tobie shook her head. "You don't know that, Maggie."

"I know it in my heart," she said, guiding Tobie's hand to her chest and pulling her forward so that their lips touched in a brief kiss. "And if I haven't said it yet, thank you for saving me. I could have lain in that field for days before anyone found me."

Tobie leaned forward for a second kiss, this time not so brief. She sighed when she sat back. "I don't know what to do about that horse." Her gaze searched Maggie's. "And I don't know what to do about you, Wild Maggie."

Maggie sighed, still clasping Tobie's hand to her chest. "Same here, Tobie Mason. But right now, I need to take my pills and get some sleep. I'm exhausted from lugging this cast out to the barn and back."

"I'll get you some water."

Maggie reluctantly released Tobie's hand. She raised her voice so Tobie could hear her from the kitchen. "Cindy cleaned the guest room for you so you could sleep in a real bed tonight."

Tobie returned with a bottle of water. "I'd rather sleep on the sofa again…uh, you know, so I can check Heart's stall camera…and you during the night."

Maggie smiled. "I guess you don't mind my snoring, then. These pain pills knock me on my ass."

"Not if you don't mind mine," Tobie said, smiling back.

She excused herself to the bathroom to get ready for bed, and Maggie couldn't help cracking an eye open to take in Tobie's long, toned legs when she returned wearing boxers and a T-shirt.

"Night, Maggie," Tobie said softly.

"Good night," she said, smiling again into the darkness.

Chapter Sixteen

Heart was stiff the next day, so Tobie walked her slowly around the paddock after checking her wound and changing her bandage. The area near her teats was still draining, but Dr. Weston had warned them that would be normal, and the drainage didn't look infected. Penny came over from the adjoining pasture to greet Heart and walked the fence line with them, as if lending support to her wounded friend.

They were on their second trek around the small paddock when a loud neigh rang out from the edge of the forest beyond Penny's pasture. Heart stopped and lifted her head, then answered back, bobbing her head impatiently.

"That's Night calling for his new mare," Maggie said.

Tobie nearly jumped out of her skin. She'd been so intent on Heart's movement that she hadn't heard Maggie approach.

"He'd come this close to a farm for one mare?"

"I grow hay on the unfenced back acres, but I always take only one cutting. The second cutting is left for the wild horses to graze when the greenery at their usual spots dies out for the winter. So they're not afraid to come fairly close to the farm buildings." Maggie shrugged. "Still, he seems unusually attached to her. Maybe she is carrying his baby."

Tobie snorted. "I've never heard of stallions showing any indication they're aware of a mare carrying their offspring."

"There's a lot we don't know about horses in their natural world. Did you know that they group together like families? It's not just stallions that fight for possession of mares. Less-dominant colts are allowed to stay with their herd as long as they don't try to breed the mares or challenge the stallion. They'll band together to face enemies when cornered and can recognize each other even after being separated for years. And there's so much more left to learn about them."

Heart whinnied again, and Night answered. Kate looked toward the woods and barked.

"I better get her back inside before she gets too worked up and pops some stitches," Tobie said, leading Heart into the barn again.

Maggie and Kate followed Tobie into the barn. "What are you planning to do when she's healed?"

"She doesn't belong to me. I'll have to turn her over to the insurance company."

"She deserves to be free, Tobie."

"What, so she can get hurt again? If I hadn't found her, she would have died a painful death." Tobie slammed the stall door closed and latched it. "She's got great bloodlines. Someone looking for a hunter-jumper or someone who will breed her and won't mind hand-raising her baby if it gives them the chance to own a superior racehorse would be glad to have her."

"And how are you going to make sure of that? Once the insurance company gets its hands on her, you won't have any say in what happens to her. Besides, once scar tissue develops on that belly wound, she might not be able to compete in jumping competitions."

Misery and indecision filled Tobie. She whirled on Maggie. "You think I can just let her go? The insurance company would come after me. They'd sue me for everything I have. And that's not much. My truck, that fancy trailer, and a smaller trailer I left back in Kentucky are the only things I own. I'll have nothing."

"You'll have me, and this farm." Maggie looked as if her declaration surprised her as much as it did Tobie, like she wanted to slap a hand over her own mouth.

"Oh, Maggie. We've known each other what? A little over two weeks?"

Maggie turned and headed back to the house as fast as she could on crutches, Kate following close behind.

Tobie slapped herself on the forehead. "Shit. Wait, Maggie. Just wait." She watched Maggie and kicked at the dusty barn floor. "Damn it. Why do I always fuck things up?"

❖

Maggie waited dinner for more than an hour, but when it didn't seem Tobie was coming back to the house, she sat in front of her trail monitors and ate a bowl of the vegetable soup she'd thawed from the freezer. The herds seemed to have weathered the latest storm well and were moving about their usual feeding grounds. Night's group had already migrated to Maggie's far pastures to graze the rich hay.

The herds were fine, she'd pretty much put up all the food she'd need for winter, and bills were paid, donations rolling in through the website to fund a contraception project for the wild herds. So why was she so miserable? It was that damned Tobie Mason. She wished she'd never met her. Maggie closed her eyes, and visions of those long, bare legs when Tobie walked around in her boxers caused strange sensations in her belly. Wonderful sensations. Damn it.

A light tap, tap on the door interrupted Maggie's ruminations. She steeled herself. "Come on in."

Tobie, eyes downcast and feet shuffling like she was walking toward her execution, inched in.

"Vegetable soup's still hot on the stove, and biscuits are warming in the oven." She kept her eyes on the monitors.

"Maggie—"

"I wasn't suggesting anything, Tobie. You wouldn't be the first homeless stray I've picked up and helped get back on their feet. Just ask Ricky or Cindy." She didn't look up, even during the long minutes of foot-shuffling that followed.

Tobie finally spoke. "Do you kiss all your homeless strays?"

Maggie snorted and looked up to meet Tobie's gaze. "No. I didn't kiss any of them."

"Then why me?"

She fidgeted in her seat, pretending to scan the monitors again before answering. "Shit. It's because of those soulful brown eyes, long, toned legs, and sexy ass. Hard to ignore."

Tobie's smile began small, then stretched into a toothy grin. "You think I have a cute ass?"

"Don't tell me you didn't already know that."

"Well, it is behind me, so I don't see it much." Tobie walked around the table to kneel beside Maggie's chair. "Besides, I've been too captivated by those beautiful blue eyes of yours to notice anything else. You can't tell me you didn't already know what a weapon they are."

"Weapon?"

"One minute they're warm, blue sky and the next, hot lasers."

"Well, I—" Maggie stuttered, unsure how to respond. "I just am who I am."

Tobie's hand was hot on her cheek. "I love who you are, Maggie, as much as I know about you. I'm so sorry about my response in the barn. I'm not used to anyone opening their home to me like you have. I've always been on my own. My grandmother gave me a place to live and food to eat after my parents died, but she wasn't a warm person. I think she left her farm to me because I was her only living relative. She wasn't unkind, but she wasn't very soft. So I don't always know how to handle a compliment or an offer of affection."

Maggie reached up to clasp the hand caressing her cheek and kissed the back of it. "Truthfully, you've stirred up feelings I haven't felt for a long time. I'm not sure how to respond either. I don't intend to rope you into anything. And you don't owe me a thing for staying here. Having you here is helping me."

"I can do more, if you'll show me how while Heart heals."

"You might regret offering after a lesson in milking rambunctious goats and collecting eggs from cranky hens."

Tobie chuckled as she stood. "Want some more soup while I get some?"

"About half a bowl, and another biscuit, please."

"Coming right up."

They settled at the table with their dinner, watched the trail monitors, and Maggie explained her wild horse project to Tobie. Her website had more than a million followers, as well as sponsors, and solicited donations to help with the research. She explained the need to push contraception programs to control the wild horse population, while the government just wanted to round them up and sell them off.

"Sorry. I tend to get carried away when I talk about the project. I don't know what I'd have done without Ricky. He set up this whole website and helped me install and link up the trail cameras. The boy is a tech genius. He could be working for big corporations, pulling down a huge salary. But he only wants to raise a family in this little town. That's something special, you know, to realize what makes you happy and shut out all the voices saying you're not living up to your potential."

"It takes a lot of courage. I guess I never had to deal with pressure to be anything. Nobody ever expected anything from me, so it was up to me whether I became successful or not."

They were both quiet a while, eating their soup and biscuits.

"I know you have a sister, but what about the rest of your family?" Tobie asked.

"I grew up two steps behind my dad. He taught me about farming, raising cattle, and riding horses. My mother's dad passed this farm down to her and my father. Mom died of ovarian cancer before I left for college and discovered I like girls rather than boys. I don't know if it was Mom's absence or my sexual orientation, but things weren't the same between Dad and me. That's probably why I stayed until I finished my doctorate. Then I came home with a lot of ideas about organic farming and diversifying with dairy goats, but Dad was a traditionalist. He'd say, 'You can do all that after I'm dead and buried.' So, I did. He was barely in the ground before I sold off the cattle, started the goat dairy, and switched from growing feed corn to growing sorghum."

"Ever thought about cannabis for a cash crop? It is legal in this state now."

"Too much trouble. It takes tons of paperwork, and then you grow it and every teenager in the county is sneaking into your fields at night to steal a plant or two, so you have to hire security. Nobody tries to swipe sorghum. Hell, most people don't know what to do with it, but it's like soybeans and peanuts—it has a million uses."

"Good point." Tobie took their bowls to the sink and rinsed

them before placing them in the dishwasher. "Recliner again tonight?"

"No, uh, my butt's getting sore from being on my back all the time. I'm usually a side sleeper, so I'm going to try the bed tonight."

"Okay. Can I do anything to help?"

"You go ahead and get ready for bed. I'll holler if I need help."

Tobie had barely stepped out of the bathroom when she heard a faint "Need a little help, please." She found Maggie struggling to tuck pillows around the casted leg and pull up the bed covers. "What's the problem here?" She was trying not to laugh at Maggie's predicament. She had covers snagged on the toe of her cast and pillows tucked everywhere. "What are you trying to do?"

"I have to lie on this side, because this heavy cast crushes my good leg if I lie on the other one, but I need something to rest against to keep from rolling over onto my face. These feather pillows just aren't firm enough." She scowled as she threw one off the bed, and Tobie caught it.

Maggie's battle with the pillows stopped suddenly, her gaze hot as it focused on Tobie's legs and slowly traveled upward. Tobie gave her a smug smile to let her know she was aware that she was being cruised.

She lifted the covers, freeing where they were snagged on Maggie's cast, then climbed into the bed and held her arm out.

"What are you doing?" Maggie blinked a few times.

Tobie patted her shoulder. "Giving you something more solid to prop against." She scooted closer to Maggie. "I'm a back sleeper most of the time anyway. You can put your other leg on mine, and rest your head right here," she said, patting her shoulder again.

"I don't know if this is a good idea," Maggie said.

Tobie wanted to laugh at Maggie's wary expression. "It's a great idea. Now stop fussing and snuggle in. I promise to be good... unless you don't want me to."

"Cheeky, aren't you?"

"I've been accused of it before, but I plead the Fifth."

Kate jumped onto the bed and looked puzzled for a minute before hopping over their legs and curling up against Maggie's other side. Then Maggie caved and snuggled against Tobie's side, resting her head in the well of Tobie's shoulder. They both heaved big sighs.

"This feels good," Tobie whispered into the dark.

"Mmm" was Maggie's only response before she drifted off.

CHAPTER SEVENTEEN

Maggie fidgeted on the doctor's table. "I'm tired of waiting. Just hand me that saw and see if you can figure out how to turn it on."

Tobie laughed. "I will not. You've had that cast on for nearly two weeks. You can wait a few more minutes."

"It itches, damn it." It had been driving her crazy for days.

After a quick rap on the door, Dr. Oh answered her complaint. "And you can scratch as much as you want as soon as I cut that off."

"Thank God, Doc. She was about to take that saw in her own hands," Tobie said.

Maggie scowled at the doctor. "I've been waiting forever."

"You've been waiting fifteen minutes, Maggie Wilkes, while I cut the cast off an adorable five-year-old with a brilliant smile. She gave me a kiss on the cheek for removing her cast. My staff tells me you've never shown that kind of appreciation to Dr. Berger."

"There have been others?" Tobie asked.

The nurse that followed Dr. Oh into the room spoke up. "Oh, yeah. I was fresh out of nursing school when she broke her arm trying to ride a cow because her father wouldn't buy her a pony." She winked at Maggie. "And I helped cast the other arm when she fell off the horse that he finally did buy her."

"How was I to know a cowpony wouldn't make a good show jumper?"

The doctor shook his head as he chuckled and fired up the saw. A few minutes later, the cast cracked open and revealed two weeks of sweat, dead skin, and unshaven leg. A long line of stitches ran from the right of her shin to the back of her calf.

"Jesus, that stinks." Maggie wrinkled her nose, but Tobie leaned closer to inspect it.

"Looks good," the doctor said, squinting at the stitches while a nurse cleaned her leg with an alcohol swab. He reached for a suture removal kit. "Let's get those stitches out so you can go home and take a long bath." He seemed pleased when he finished. "I still don't want you putting weight on that leg yet. I sewed a lot of muscle back together, and it needs more time to heal. I'm going to put you in a boot to keep those muscles flexed a while longer. You can take it off to bathe but keep it on all night so that you don't unconsciously flex that calf." The nurse appeared with a compression sock and a boot with Velcro straps, and he strapped it into place. "I want to see you in a week to determine if you can start physical therapy."

"How long do I have to wear this boot?"

"Probably no more than a couple of weeks. You can hobble around the house without the crutches while you have the boot on, but I don't want you walking on that leg much yet. You could tear some of the work I did inside."

Tobie handed Maggie her crutches. "Thanks, Doc. I'll bring her back in a week."

❖

"Do you want to stop at the diner?" Tobie asked as she drove them from the hospital.

Maggie frowned. "No. I want to go straight home and have a long soak in the bathtub." It was impossible to take a bath with a full cast, and even trying to wrap it in plastic for a shower couldn't stop water from draining down her leg. Leaning over the tub to wash her hair and washing up in the sink were not meeting her need to feel clean.

Tobie flashed her a smile. "Your wish is my command."

They'd slept together every night for the past week but had stopped at kissing and a little heavy petting. Maggie thought she was going to burst if Tobie didn't make a move soon. Still uncertain about their age difference, she'd held back, telling herself she wanted to be fully mobile before things went any further between them. And maybe Tobie was holding back because she didn't plan to stay. Or maybe Tobie wasn't as experienced as Maggie and was waiting for her to make the first move. Or maybe Tobie wasn't as interested as Maggie was.

"Let me help you inside," Tobie said when they arrived back at the farm.

"I've got it. Make yourself a sandwich if you're hungry. I plan to have a good, long soak."

Tobie jogged ahead and held the door open for her since she was still on crutches. "Are you sure you can get that boot off by yourself?"

"I'm sure. It's not the first time I've had to wear one."

"Are you that accident-prone?"

"No. I used to do a little rodeoing, and other times I got hurt, I was doing something I shouldn't...like trying to get a cowpony to jump a four-foot fence because I was ten years old and decided I wanted to be in the Olympics."

"That would do it."

"Didn't you get injured when you were growing up?"

"Only once. We didn't have health insurance, so Grandma got some supplies out of her veterinary truck and stitched me up at home the first time I cut myself playing outside. I was more careful after that and learned how to use Steri-Strips and ice to hide any injuries."

"Damn. How old were you?"

"Thirteen. Fortunately, I never broke any bones that needed repair."

"No kidding." Maggie went into the bathroom to put her razor and shaving cream in the tray next to the tub. "You can help by getting a clean towel and a bath bomb from the hall closet. And maybe some fresh sweats and a T-shirt from that stack of clothes on my dresser."

Tobie could hear the water running when she returned with the requested items and hesitated when she saw the pile of clothes and discarded boot on the floor, then nearly swallowed her tongue at the sight of Maggie's bare back and bottom as she sat on the side of the tub, shaving away two weeks of hair growth. She covered her eyes and felt her way to a chair next to the tub, where she placed the clothes and towel. "I, uh, didn't know if you wanted undies, but I brought a pair anyway."

"Thanks. Can you reach up and get the shower head for me so I can rinse off? I want to wash all this hair down the drain before I fill the tub for a soak."

Tobie groaned and grappled for the handheld showerhead while keeping her eyes covered with her hand. "You're going to kill me, woman."

Maggie laughed. "Haven't you seen a naked woman before?"

"Not the woman who's been sleeping on my shoulder each night and fueling my wet dreams," Tobie said.

Maggie put the razor aside and plugged the drain, then lowered herself into the tub. "You smell like goats from milking this morning. I think you need to get in here with me. I could use someone to lean back on."

"Just anyone?" Tobie was only teasing because she was already half out of her clothes. When she was fully naked, she paused for a minute to let Maggie take her in.

"Only the woman who's been fueling my wet dreams," Maggie said.

Tobie slid in behind Maggie, who tossed the lavender bath bomb into the water. Her nipples were hard against Maggie's back, and she wrapped her arms around Maggie to pull her closer. She couldn't resist stealing a few kisses along the graceful curve of Maggie's neck and shoulder, wanting to go slow and unsure if there were boundaries to the invitation to bathe together.

As the long, claw-foot tub filled with warm water, Maggie laid her head back on Tobie's shoulder and idly stroked Tobie's legs that stretched out on either side of her.

"You're killing me, Mags," Tobie whispered in her ear.

"Shush," Maggie said. "Just relax for a bit."

They lay in the tub until the hot water was exhausted, trading occasional kisses. Tobie smoothed her hands up Maggie's ribs to cup her small breasts. "You are a beautiful woman, Maggie Wilkes."

"Take me to bed, Tobie Mason."

❖

Calling on all her strength, Tobie rose from the tub and lifted Maggie into her arms, carrying her across the hall to their bed. She laid her gently onto the patchwork quilt. Her back muscles would pay later for that romantic feat. Then she kissed her long and deep before backing away. "I'll be right back," she said.

Maggie grimaced when she returned with a sock and the boot and strapped it to her foot. "That's not very sexy," Maggie complained.

She caressed Maggie's cheek. "You would be sexy even if you were still in that full leg cast. I'd never forgive myself if we reinjured your leg when your recovery is going so well." Then she stretched out beside her, both groaning as the full length of their bodies made contact. "You are the most beautiful woman I've ever known." She captured Maggie's gaze as she stroked down her side and across her belly. "I was captured by those blue eyes that first day we met in the middle of a storm with my trailer stuck in the mud and my horse running away. All I could think about was the stunning color of your eyes."

Maggie pulled her down and took her mouth in a kiss both tender and ferocious. She tugged Tobie on top of her and gripped her buttocks as Tobie undulated against her. "Tobie, Tobie," she moaned.

"Tell me what you need," Tobie whispered.

"I need your mouth on me," Maggie said, pressing down on her shoulders.

Tobie kissed her way along Maggie body. "I love your belly, so firm yet soft."

Maggie scoffed. "Don't you mean my middle-age spread?"

"Especially that, because it makes you real instead of a goddess I'd be afraid to approach."

She moved up and sucked Maggie's small breast, raking her teeth gently against the hard nipple and drawing a gasp from Maggie before moving quickly to shoulder between her legs. Her senses were filled with Maggie's scent, the salty taste of her on her tongue, and the clench of Maggie's belly as she teased the hard bundle of sensitive nerves. She'd vowed to take her time, but the hard clit in her mouth and the fingers digging into her hair filled her with an urgency to claim this woman, to make her scream with pleasure. One stroke, two strokes—then she sucked hard, and Maggie's orgasm pulsed in her mouth.

"Fuck," Maggie yelled when Tobie inserted one finger, then two and stroked her to a second climax.

When Maggie stilled, Tobie surged forward, sliding her sopping sex against Maggie's good leg. "I am so wet for you," she said, pumping against her. "You make me so hard."

Maggie slid her fingers between her leg and Tobie's sex, massaging her clit only a stroke or two before an orgasm slammed into her, bowing her body and twisting her insides in exquisite pleasure. "Oh, God. Oh, Maggie." She collapsed at last on top of Maggie, their bodies slick with sweat but smelling of the lavender bath bomb.

They'd barely had time to catch their breath when someone flung the bedroom door open.

"Oh my God. What in the hell is going on here?" Maggie's sister, Judy, stood in the doorway, her eyes wide but not looking away from their naked bodies.

Maggie quickly flicked the sheet over to cover them, and Tobie slid off to the side of her. "What the hell, Judy. Don't you know how to knock?"

Judy huffed but made no move to leave the room. "I thought someone was being hurt back here with all the, uh, noise. Have you no decency? It's the middle of the day."

"Have you no decency? Get out of my bedroom."

"Cindy sent you dinner from the diner," Judy declared, then backed out of the room and slammed the door. Maggie looked at Tobie, and they both laughed.

"Who the hell is that?" Tobie glared at the door.

"That was my infamous sister, Judy, Ricky's mother."

"So much for languishing in the afterglow or moving on to round two."

Maggie stroked her hand along Tobie's naked shoulder and down her side. "Hold on to that idea. We'll have time later," she said. "We have to milk, feed, and bed the livestock down anyway." She sat up to swing her legs to the floor. "That's the downside of owning a farm. The work never stops. Help me get some pants over this boot."

Despite Maggie's matter-of-fact listing of chores, they paused here and there for a shy kiss or caress as they helped each other dress. When they were presentable, they both took a deep breath and headed for the kitchen.

Judy stood over three foam containers, hands on her hips. "I can't believe you are rolling around in the bed with that girl."

"This girl is a thirty-four-year-old woman," Tobie said, joining them in the kitchen and standing up to Judy. "And we are both consenting adults. I didn't realize Maggie needed your permission."

Judy ignored Tobie and turned on Maggie. "It's a sin, Maggie Wilkes. Pastor John has preached about the sins of lying with the same sex. You know that. What would Mama say if she knew you were...were...having sex with another woman?"

"She would say you and Pastor John need to mind your own business." Maggie crutched over to the table and opened one of the containers. "Yum. Fried chicken. I can always count on Cindy." She wanted Tobie to see that Judy's preaching was nothing but the usual hot air. "Tobie, can you pour us some iced tea?"

Tobie clearly picked up on Maggie's nonchalance toward Judy's aggression. "I see three dinners. Are you staying to eat with us, Judy? What would you like to drink?"

Judy sputtered at Tobie's pleasant question. "Well, I didn't know if Ricky might be here. That dinner is for him." She snatched it up. "He must be working, so I guess I'll take it by the sheriff's office." She left in a huff, her nose in the air as if she smelled something bad.

Maggie looked at Tobie as they listened to Judy's car spin its wheels leaving the driveway, and they laughed. She hadn't laughed so much in years and loved that she and Tobie laughed together a lot.

"Your sister is a piece of work," Tobie said, digging into her fried chicken and mashed potatoes.

"She's free entertainment, that's for sure," Maggie said. "Actually, though, if you can put up with her preaching, she'll be the first in your corner if you need something."

"Good to know," Tobie said. They were quiet for a long minute, enjoying their chicken dinners. "Cindy is sure around a lot to help you," she said, avoiding Maggie's gaze. Tobie's statement shouted insecurity.

"Cindy and I have a history, but that's exactly what it is—history. We were kids then, and she's happily married now. We're still good friends, and I count her husband, Jake, as one of my best friends, too." Maggie wanted to reassure Tobie, but she had some insecurities of her own. "How's Heart look today? Have you talked to the insurance guy lately?"

"No, but she's healing well. That one pocket of infection looks good since Dr. Weston drained it." Tobie took a bite of chicken and chewed. "Night keeps showing up most days. I figured he'd lose interest, but it's been two weeks."

"Did Dr. Weston ultrasound her?"

"No. It's still early."

"Don't you want to know before you turn her over to them?"

Tobie put her fork down. "I don't know what I want to do."

"What if you could buy her from the insurance company?"

"Where am I going to get that kind of money? She was insured for a million, and her sell price was eighty thousand."

"Can I show you something?" Maggie asked.

"Sure."

They were already seated at the table, where Maggie kept her laptop connected to two other monitors to keep track of the trail monitors. She switched one screen to her website, logging in as an administrator. "I didn't want to go live with this until you okayed it, but Ricky made this video to help raise money for Heart's purchase, if you agree."

She clicked on a video, and it began with footage of Sarah's Heart winning her last race. A narrator introduced the story of the Thoroughbred mare that loved nothing more than to run, and then it switched to a clip from the television segment with Sarah Carmichael.

"She loves to run so much," Sarah said to the interviewer, "that I believe she'd still race around the track if she were the only horse out there."

"You've told us that you have a fatal illness, but you're not afraid of dying."

"No. I'm at peace with it. I've lived past my life expectancy already, and I'm grateful for that because these last few years brought Heart into my life. When she runs, she looks so free. My father can't talk about it, but when I think of death, I imagine being free of this disease that has restricted everything I can do. I dream of running across the field with Heart, the wind in our faces, and nothing holding us back. I hope she'll always be free to run."

The next clip was of the news reports about the accident when Heart escaped. Even a brief clip of Heart running with the wild herd and grazing at Night's side was included. The narrator explained that Heart had been injured and was recovering. The buyer had already collected on her insurance policy, so the insurance company now owned her and could do what they wanted with her as soon as she healed.

Then Maggie appeared on-camera. "Sarah Carmichael died a month after that news feature, but her dream of running free with her beloved mare still lives. Help us raise the funds to buy Sarah's Heart and return her to the wild herd, where she can run free like Sarah Carmichael wanted. Your donations, made through this website to support wild horses, will be tax-deductible."

Tobie was quiet for a while. "I don't know what to say. That's amazing work."

"Ricky's a genius with this computer stuff."

Tobie shook her head. "I can see you raising ten, maybe twenty thousand, but eighty thousand dollars is a lot of money. And there's no guarantee the insurance company will sell her, even if we do get the money."

"This won't go on just my website. It will be posted on TikTok, Instagram, Facebook, and Twitter, uh, X, Ricky says. I didn't believe in the power to raise money on social media, but Ricky proved me wrong. How do you think I maintain these trail cameras and spend time documenting the movements of the wild horse herds? The farm provides only about half my income. Donations to my wild horses' fund supplies the rest."

Tobie sat back in her chair and pushed the remains of her dinner away. "If you do raise enough money and I accept it, I still might not want to let her go free. She's already been injured once. She could get hurt again."

Maggie drew her chair next to Tobie's and kissed her briefly.

"Life is full of maybes, Tobie. You have to let go sometimes and let life happen. If you don't, you might dodge some of life's hurts, but you also could miss out on some happiness, too."

Tobie searched her eyes. "I'm not good at letting go. I need to be in control to protect myself because no one else has ever looked out for me." She glanced away, drumming her fingers on the table in an uneven pattern. "On the other hand, if I did manage to buy her from the insurance company, they would make some of the money they paid out and maybe not cancel my policy."

"So, can Ricky make this video live?"

Tobie was quiet for a few minutes, and Maggie could see the struggle in her eyes. Finally, she nodded. "Yeah. What the hell? It's worth a try."

"I want you to see something," Tobie said, waking Maggie several weeks later.

"What? Is something wrong?"

"No. Just come outside with me."

"Are you nuts? We've got another hour or two to sleep."

"Do you trust me?"

"I don't know if I should trust a lunatic who wakes me up in the middle of the night to go outside." Despite her protest, Maggie rose, donned the robe Tobie held out for her, and grabbed her crutches. "Let's see. It's not lambing season, so no goat babies are due, and I can't imagine you'd get me up at this hour to see chicks hatch."

"Just come with me."

The night was clear and the sky star-studded. She led Maggie over to a folding chaise lounge, settled herself in the chair, then helped Maggie lower herself and position her booted foot so she sat between Tobie's legs and leaned against her chest.

"Why are we sitting in the cold when we could be in my warm bed?"

Tobie unfolded a blanket and tucked it around them. She kissed down Maggie's neck and breathed in her ear. "Just wait for it."

A short time later, when Maggie was about to doze off, the sky seemed to rain stars, streaking across the sky. Tobie spoke softly in her ear. "The stars are falling down from the sky, Maggie Wilkes, because they want to be close to you."

Maggie smiled up at the meteor shower. "Huh. Did you forget how old I am and think I wouldn't know you plagiarized that idea from an old pop song?"

"It's true, Maggie. About the stars. I haven't met one person in town who thinks you're less than a goddess."

Maggie scoffed. "You obviously haven't talked to any of the BLM guys. They think I'm Satan incarnate."

"I see starlight every time I look into your blue eyes," Tobie whispered, accenting her words with more neck kisses.

"I'm sure that's not the song I'm thinking of." Maggie gasped. When Tobie sucked on her pulse, she reached for the arms of the lounger and hit the release to lay the chair flat. Then she twisted so that she was face-to-face with Tobie.

Tobie's mouth was warm, her tongue soft but insistent. She spread her legs, drawing Maggie closer, tighter against her. Maggie slid her hands under Tobie's long-sleeved T-shirt and palmed her breasts. She tweaked her nipples and smiled at the hitch in Tobie's breath.

"We can go inside," Tobie choked out, moaning when Maggie found and tickled her navel with her tongue.

"Too late," Maggie said, sliding lower. It was awkward with her boot hanging off the end of the chaise, but she was determined to have her mouth on Tobie, to taste her, to bring her to a screaming climax.

She pushed Tobie's shirt up, exposing her breasts and belly to the cold night air, then licked her way down, raising goosebumps on both of her arms.

"Please, Mags, don't tease." She could feel Tobie's stomach muscles tighten and her legs tense. Then she screamed up at the stars streaking across the midnight-black sky. Maggie was smug as she crawled back up to face Tobie, who was sweaty and still panting. She could feel Tobie's heart pounding in her chest.

"Did I wreck your plans to have your way with me?" she asked.

"Not in the least," Tobie said, blowing out a few calming breaths to slow her heart. "There's always payback." She glided her hand down between Maggie's legs and swiftly entered her with one, then two fingers. She massaged her engorged clit with the heel of her hand as Maggie groaned, then rocked up and down on Tobie's fingers. "That's it, babe. Come for me."

Maggie's eyes widened and she shuddered. Tobie worked her hand to milk every ounce of her climax until Maggie collapsed on top of her.

"I can't get enough of you," Maggie whispered into Tobie's shoulder.

Tobie chuckled. "I keep expecting your sister to drive up and say, 'Oh my God. They're doing it in the yard now.'"

Maggie laughed, too, then quieted.

They lay in silence, their hearts beating together under the blanket. When Maggie's breathing evened out, Tobie realized she'd fallen asleep. Smiling to herself, Tobie tucked the blanket around them and closed her eyes while the sun began to peek over the mountains and cast a dazzling display of color across the farm's fields.

CHAPTER EIGHTEEN

Maggie nearly jumped up from her recliner where she was resting her leg and getting in an afternoon nap while Tobie sat on the couch doing the paperwork for her upcoming travel schedule.

"What is it?" Tobie asked, also standing but not knowing why.

Maggie scrambled for her crutches at the now audible *whoop-whoop* of a helicopter. "Goddamned BLM idiots. I've told them not to fly over my farm." She ditched one of her crutches for a rifle propped in the corner of the kitchen.

"Whoa," Tobie said. "You can't shoot at them. You don't own the airspace."

But Maggie wasn't listening. She hobbled out the back door with Kate on her heels, barking up at the helicopter.

Tobie barely had time to find her boots and slip them on before Maggie had reached the equipment barn. She jogged to catch up and arrived as Maggie was climbing into a Gator, John Deere's version of a farm all-terrain vehicle. Kate hopped into the back as Tobie pushed Maggie to the passenger side. "I'll drive," she said. "You'll wreck trying to push the pedal with your left foot. Where are we going?"

"Take that tractor path alongside the goats' pasture. We're headed to the back pastures. And hurry."

They bumped over the rutted path and through a section of forest before bursting onto a huge plain of waving grass. The helicopter hovered over the field as two families of wild horses began to melt into the surrounding woods. One horse, a muscular brown-and-white pinto stallion, reared and pawed at the sky as if he could fight the sky predator.

"Stop here," Maggie said. She was climbing out of the Gator before Tobie could come to a full stop.

"Maggie, wait." Tobie and Kate hurried after her as she hobbled over to something covered with a small tarp. She flung the tarp aside to expose a skeet launcher.

The helicopter appeared to leave but hovered low over the trees where the horses had taken shelter. Terrified horses reemerged from the woods, chased by the helicopter that seemed to be herding them toward a path at the other end of the field.

Maggie took up position next to the already loaded skeet launcher. "Pull, Kate."

Tobie watched in amazement as Kate rounded the launcher and stepped on a button that shot a clay target into the sky, a few feet from the helicopter.

Maggie took aim and pulled the trigger. The target exploded, and the helicopter jerked away from the flying pieces.

"Maggie, you can't shoot at them," Tobie wondered how many years you could get in prison if you hit a federal helicopter.

"I'm not shooting at them. I'm shooting skeet on my own property." She reached down to adjust the launcher to intercept the path of the helicopter. "Pull, Kate."

Kate stepped on the button, and another clay target shot up. Maggie waited until it was fully airborne and near the front of the helicopter, then took aim and fired. The target exploded all over the windshield of the chopper and stopped any forward movement. "Pull, Kate."

Again a target flew into the air, and Maggie nailed it again, inches in front of the helicopter. The chopper hovered another few seconds before landing softly on the grass, and its blades slowed.

The pilot's movements were quick and angry as he unbuckled his flight harness and jumped out to stride across the field to Maggie.

"Son of a bitch," he shouted before he ever reached them. Tobie moved to stand protectively by Maggie's side. "One more shot at my helicopter, and I'll call the sheriff again. I guess that one night you spent in jail wasn't enough."

"I don't know what you mean," Maggie said, smiling while she reloaded her shotgun. "I'm on my own property, shooting skeet. It's not my fault you were flying so low over my farm."

"Damn it, woman. You nearly hit me. I could have crashed."

"I hit my target. I can't help it if you flew into its path."

"I'm calling the sheriff."

"Go ahead, because I'd like him to charge you with trespassing on my property. Then we'll see who spends the night in jail." She held out her hand. "In fact, give me the keys to that helicopter. I'm confiscating it for being on my land without my permission."

The man began backing up. "Ha. Shows what you know. Helicopters aren't cars. They don't need keys to start."

"Put your hands up." Maggie leveled her shotgun at the man.

The man scoffed. "You won't shoot me. I'm part of a government operation to round up these horses."

Maggie fired one barrel of the double-barrel shotgun. Buckshot sprayed the ground in front of the man, and his arms shot skyward.

"You're crazy, lady."

"Tobie, get his keys."

Tobie moved quickly and found a set of keys in the man's pocket. She held them up. "He says the chopper doesn't use keys."

"I'm very familiar with their helicopters. Keys don't start it, but they do lock the doors so it can't be stolen when left unattended."

Tobie nodded and went to the helicopter, finding the right key, then locking the doors. She took the small key from his key ring, then returned the other ones to his pocket. She gave the small key to Maggie.

"Thanks. Can you call 9-1-1, please, and tell them I'm holding a trespasser until they come get him?"

"Maggie. I don't know about this."

"I do. Make the call, please, or I will."

Tobie was connected to the local dispatcher.

"This is the sheriff's department. What's your emergency?"

Maggie held out her hand without taking her eyes off the pilot, and Tobie gave her the phone. "Beth, this is Maggie Wilkes. I caught a trespasser on my property, and I'm holding him until you send someone to pick him up."

"Oh my God, Ms. Maggie. Are you hurt? Do you need medical assistance?"

"No, but tell Sheriff Chandler that he needs to bring a flatbed trailer. I've confiscated this guy's transportation, and it will need to be hauled to the compound lot."

"I'll send Johnny out with his tow truck."

"Nope. It's not a car he can tow. It's a helicopter, so unless you have someone who can fly it to the compound lot, then you need to send a flatbed."

"Ms. Maggie. Are you messing with those government people again? You haven't shot anybody, have you?"

"Not yet. But you need to send the sheriff before I lose my patience and fill him full of buckshot."

"Right away. The sheriff's here and putting his hat on now."

"Thank you. Tell him we're in the back pastures. He can drive to us on the tractor path that runs by the goat pasture."

The sheriff answered this time. "For God's sake, Maggie. When are you going to leave those men alone? They're just doing their job."

"When they leave me alone and stop flying low and trying to chase horses off my farm. It upsets my chickens so they won't lay and scared Penny so much she nearly ran into a fence."

"Nothing has ever scared that mule."

"I'm out here shooting skeet, Sheriff, so you better come get him before I accidentally shoot the pilot."

"Hang on. I'll be there in ten."

Tobie edged closer and whispered, "Have you ever shot anyone?"

"Nope." She gestured at the pilot. "But he doesn't know that."

Tobie raised her voice so the man could hear. "You might as well sit. The sheriff's on his way."

"Good. Maybe he'll haul this crazy woman away." The pilot kept grumbling but sat where he stood.

A second helicopter appeared over the trees and hovered there, the pilot likely assessing the situation on the ground.

Maggie shouldered the shotgun and called out, "Pull, Kate."

The dog stepped on the button again, and a clay target headed skyward. Maggie pulled the trigger, and the target exploded like the others. "Five times regional champion," she told Tobie.

The second helicopter pilot seemed to think twice about intervening and turned back.

❖

"Maggie, Maggie, Maggie. You can't keep doing this." Sheriff Dan Chandler helped the pilot up. "Go sit in the back of my cruiser," he told the man.

"That dog has been staring at me the whole time. It'll bite me if I move."

Chandler closed his eyes and heaved a sigh. "Kate is a herding dog. She won't bite you, but she will herd you away from Maggie."

"That crazy woman was shooting at me," the pilot said. "She nearly made me crash."

"I don't want to handcuff you," Chandler said. "But I will if you don't go ahead and get in that police cruiser. It appears that you have trespassed on her property, so unless you want to spend a night in jail for resisting arrest, then you better do what I say."

The pilot shook his head but started toward the sheriff's vehicle. When he turned around to say something else, Kate darted forward and nipped at his foot.

He danced away and walked faster toward the cruiser. "I thought you said she didn't bite."

"I reckon there's a first time for everything," Chandler said, sounding like an aggravated parent teaching a child a lesson. He turned back to Maggie. "Did you shoot his helicopter, Maggie?"

"I was practicing my skeet shooting when this guy shows up and keeps flying over my firing range. Then he landed in my field and accused me of shooting at him. Be my guest. Check his helicopter for any buckshot. I didn't even come close to shooting his bird."

"Well, we both know you're a sharpshooter and would have plugged him if he hadn't landed."

Tobie almost laughed when Maggie feigned surprise, a hand pressed to her chest as if in shock. "I would never."

The pilot turned back to them. "Why, you lying bitch—"

"Kate, pull two." Maggie issued the order before he had a

chance to further disparage her. Bam, bam. He turned and hurried to the police cruiser without another word.

Sheriff Chandler ducked his head to hide a smile and shook his head in surrender.

A tow truck hauling a large flatbed trailer pulled into the field and in front of the helicopter. The driver got out and spit onto the ground. He grinned, displaying teeth stained with chewing tobacco and a gap where one tooth was missing. "I see you been bird hunting again, Ms. Maggie."

"Just out shooting some skeet when I came across this guy trying to run the horses off my land."

He nodded. "Good for you. These government guys will never learn. They're always poking their noses into regular people's business."

"Don't you know it," Maggie said.

They watched as he loaded the helicopter onto the flatbed. It was obvious he'd done this before because he didn't hesitate while hooking it to a winch to pull it onto the trailer.

"Maggie, you've got to stop going after these guys," Chandler said. "I'll take him in, but he'll be out in a matter of hours and be right back on the hunt for your horses."

"I can't do anything about them chasing the horses on federal lands, but I'll keep turning them in as long as they continue to buzz my property after I've told them to stay away." Maggie hobbled over to the Gator, and Tobie could tell her leg was hurting.

Always a gentleman, Chandler helped her climb onto the Gator's seat and stowed her crutch and shotgun for her. "I'll cover up your launcher before I take him in. Y'all go on back to the house. I'll email you a court date for this guy."

"Thanks, Sheriff," Tobie said, relieved that Maggie wasn't getting arrested.

"Come shoot skeet with me sometime, Dan," Maggie said. "And tell your wife I've got some goat cheese and eggs for her whenever she wants to drop by."

"I'll do that. And I'll let Bernice know. She's been complaining about the price of eggs, so you can expect she'll come by sooner rather than later."

"Oh, and remind that boy of yours that I'll pay him if he'll stop by and cut up that oak that lightning hit the other day."

"Will do. It'll be the weekend, because this is football season, and he has practice every day after school."

"There's no rush," she said.

❖

Tobie drove the Gator to the house so Maggie wouldn't have to walk very far, then drove it to the equipment barn to stow it.

When she returned to the house, Maggie sat in her recliner, a bottle of water and Tylenol open on the table next to her. She'd refused the prescription painkillers after only a few days following her accident.

"You okay?" Tobie asked. She was both incredulous and proud of Maggie's stand against the helicopter pilot. "Aren't you afraid you'll be charged with bribing the sheriff with goat cheese and eggs?" The question wasn't serious, but she was curious.

"Yeah. Those government guys tried to pin that on me the last time I took them to court, but Dan's wife, Bernice, is my cousin. She's been getting cheese and eggs from me long before she married him, so the judge ruled they had no case."

Tobie laughed. The more she learned about this interesting woman, the more she wanted to find out. "You're something, you know."

Maggie gave her a side-eye but smiled. "I've been told that a few times, but it wasn't meant the way you say it."

"Is the whole town on your side?"

Maggie's smile vanished. "No. Not at all. I'm a thorn in the side of the cattle ranchers around here. Most of them want the wild horses gone." She was silent for a long moment. When she spoke again, her voice was soft. "I used to have a Great Pyrenees named Duke that stayed out with the goats to protect against coyotes and other predators. I had a run-in with a local rancher because his cattle wandered from federal lands onto my back pastures, and I charged him per head for the two days they grazed there. Two nights later, I woke up to gunshots, and when I ran outside, Duke was shot dead in the pasture. There was no way to prove it, but I know who did it."

"Bastards."

"That's when I started installing cameras all around my property. Then, the next time his cows wandered onto it, I charged him double. He took me to court and insisted that the judge order me to fence off my property so the cows would stay off it. The judge refused because he couldn't order me to fence anything unless I was harboring a dangerous animal."

"Has he left you alone after that?"

"He did after I asked the judge to confiscate his deer rifle so ballistics could test it against the slug Dr. Weston dug out of Duke. He had killed a valuable working farm animal.

"He told the judge that he couldn't because he'd sold that rifle. Two days later, the rifle turned up in the middle of the goat pasture, wiped clean of fingerprints, but I know it was him. He kept his face covered because I let it be known that I'd hidden cameras around the property, but he was easy enough to identify. I'd know his walk anywhere."

"I'm sorry about Duke." They shared a moment of silence in the brave dog's memory. "Are you going to get another one to guard the herd?"

"No. The cameras have motion detectors on them and buzz when they're activated at night. That gives Kate and me time to grab the shotgun and see who's out there."

Maggie turned away, as if she was looking out the newly replaced window next to her chair, but Tobie could see the tears welling in her eyes. She went to Maggie and wedged herself in the chair next to her so she could hold her.

"He was a good dog," Maggie choked out, accepting Tobie's embrace. "That bastard killed a good dog."

CHAPTER NINETEEN

"D amn. Half the county is here," Tobie said to Maggie. "Do you know the DA or the judge?"

"The assistant district attorney is a second cousin, and the judge's wife gets cheese and eggs from me. Also, her grandson can't drink cow's milk, so she gets a few bottles of goat's milk from me every month." Maggie kept her voice low.

The judge banged his gavel five or six times to quiet the overflowing courtroom. "Is the prosecution ready?" he asked when the room quieted.

"Yes, Your Honor. The prosecution is ready."

"Thank you, Mr. Brown. And the defendant?"

The helicopter pilot's lawyer stood. "The Bureau of Land Management is ready, Your Honor."

The judge banged his gavel again when the crowd booed the defense attorney. He shook his gavel at the audience. "One more outburst and I'll clear this courtroom."

The crowd quieted. Nobody wanted to miss this hearing.

The judge checked his docket, then peered at the attorney. "Have I misunderstood? The Bureau of Land Management is not the defendant in this trial. If it was, this hearing would be held in federal court, not my district court."

The attorney shifted nervously. He was young and apparently had drawn the short straw to represent the pilot. "The defendant, Mr. Hudson, was a contracted employee of and following the directions of the BLM when he was accosted by Ms. Wilkes, so we are providing representation for him."

"So noted." He consulted his docket again before addressing the pilot. "Mr. Hudson, you are charged with trespassing and going to the terror of the public. How do you plead?"

"Going to the terror of the public? I was the one terrorized," Hudson said.

"Stand up, Mr. Hudson, when you address the court. How do you plead to the charges?"

The pilot stood. "Not guilty, Your Honor."

"Then we will proceed." He looked to the prosecutor. "You have a right to a jury trial."

Hudson consulted his attorney, who stood and answered the judge. "Considering the reaction of the courtroom, I don't feel a fair and impartial jury could be found in this county. We are requesting a change of venue."

"Denied," the judge said.

"Then we will forgo a jury and trust you to administer justice according to the law."

"Good choice." He looked to the prosecutor. "Mr. Brown, do you want to explain what precipitated these charges?"

"Your Honor, Ms. Maggie Wilkes was at home, recovering from a farm equipment injury, when Mr. Hudson buzzed her farm with his helicopter several times, terrorizing her animals as well as the occupants of the house. Since the incident, her hens have laid very few eggs, and her dairy goats have given very little milk. Now, we all know that Ms. Wilkes generously supplies cheese and eggs to the local food bank and many other people in need in this community. Mr. Hudson's aggressive actions have greatly reduced her income from these products, as well as her ability to continue this act of charity."

The pilot jumped up from his chair. "The damn woman shot at me."

The judge gave three sharp raps of his gavel. "Sit down, Mr. Hudson. You will have your chance to speak when I'm done questioning Mr. Brown." He turned back to the prosecutor. "Did Ms. Wilkes shoot a gun at Mr. Hudson?"

"No, sir. Not at him."

"Could you be more specific?"

"It's true that she had a gun, but she didn't shoot it at him."

"I don't have the time or patience to pull this out of you. What did she shoot at?" He waved his gavel. "Never mind. Ms. Wilkes, I see that you're here in the courtroom. How about you come up here to the witness stand and explain what happened. Bailiff, swear her in."

Maggie hobbled up to the front of the courtroom, using both crutches that she rarely needed any more, and dutifully laid her hand on the Bible to take the oath of truth.

"Now, tell us in your own words," the judge said.

"Well, sir, I was at home in my living room when I heard the helicopter overhead. I hobbled outside as best I could and tried to calm my dairy goats and chickens that were panicked and running all over their pasture. He flew off after a few passes. Since I was up and out of the house, I had Ms. Tobie Mason, who has been helping during my convalescence, drive me out to my back acres to practice a little skeet shooting. It's been damned boring sitting around the house for weeks."

The judge nodded. "I heard you were lucky that Ms. Mason came by your farm and found you pinned down by the tractor."

"Yes, sir, I was. Very lucky."

Tobie smiled at her and caught Maggie's eye for a very small smile in return.

"So, you just happened to decide to shoot skeet after Mr. Hudson was low-flying over your farm?"

"Yes, sir. I was pretty frustrated and worked up because I've had to take the BLM to court several times to get injunctions against them chasing horses off my property. I thought shooting a few skeet would help me work off some of that anger."

"You're allowed to shoot your gun on your own property. Exactly when did you encounter Mr. Hudson again?"

"When we arrived at my back pastures where I normally practice shooting, several families of wild horses were grazing there. I hesitated then to shoot because I didn't want to spook them, but Mr. Hudson's helicopter appeared again, flying very low, and chased the horses into the woods back toward federal lands. Since the horses were leaving, I practiced a little shooting."

Hudson scoffed loudly but quieted when the judge glared at him.

"You're certain the helicopter was being flown by Mr. Hudson?"

"Yes, Your Honor. He was flying so low, he was easy to identify through the bubble windshield of the chopper. Ms. Mason was with me and can confirm that fact."

"We can hear from Ms. Mason later," the judge said. "Continue, please."

"If there was any doubt the perpetrator was Mr. Hudson, that was erased when he landed his helicopter in my field and got out to accuse me of shooting at him. I warned him that he was trespassing, but he continued toward me in a threatening manner, so I did point my gun at him then but didn't shoot at him, of course. I did confiscate the keys to his helicopter and had Ms. Mason lock it up. Then I called the sheriff to come get Mr. Hudson and his aircraft."

"Thank you, Ms. Wilkes. You can take a seat next to Mr. Brown in case I have any further questions for you."

Maggie crutched her way to the prosecutor's table, where her cousin held a chair out for her as though she were an invalid.

"Is Ms. Tobie Mason in the courtroom?"

Tobie stood and raised her hand. "Right here, Your Honor."

"Do you concur with Ms. Wilkes's recounting of what happened?"

She wanted to laugh at the informal way this judge ran his courtroom, but she schooled her face into what she hoped was an earnest expression and decided to join the circus. "Yes, sir. She was shooting skeet. She has the cutest thing set up where her dog, Kate, steps on a button to release the targets for her to shoot. She yells 'pull,' that dog steps on the button, and the targets go airborne. It's the darndest thing I've ever seen."

"I'd like to see that some time," the judge said, smiling at Tobie.

The pilot's face had become so red, he looked like he might explode.

"Okay, Mr. Hudson. Let's hear your version of what happened. Come on up so the bailiff can swear you in."

Hudson sprang from his seat and practically jogged to the witness stand. He put his hand on the Bible and sat with a triumphant expression.

"Go ahead, in your own words," the judge prompted him.

"Well, sir, the BLM contracted me to herd wild horses into a pen so a number of them could be removed from federal lands. With no natural predators, they're growing in numbers and depleting the grazing lands that other wildlife depend upon for survival."

"It's my understanding, Mr. Hudson, that the BLM allows local ranchers to graze their cattle on those same lands. Are they not guilty of depleting those same resources?"

"Those cattle feed hungry Americans, Your Honor. Since Americans have an aversion to eating horsemeat or even feeding it to their dogs, the wild horses provide nothing to the community."

A titter ran through the courtroom, and someone in the back yelled, "Is that why we stole land from the Indians? Because they didn't serve the white man's interest?"

The judge banged his gavel and glared at the crowd. "One more outburst and you're all out of here." The room went silent except for an occasional cough or sniff, and he turned back to the witness stand. "Continue, Mr. Hudson."

"I spotted two of the herds grazing in a large field next to Ms. Wilkes's farm. They were eating up her hay field, so I swooped down and herded them back toward federal property. That's when she started shooting at my helicopter, nearly causing me to crash. So, I landed and approached to inform her of the penalty for interfering with federal business. She sicced her dog on me and pointed a shotgun at me. Then she had that other woman take the keys that lock the doors of my chopper from me and called the sheriff to report me as trespassing."

"Mr. Brown, do you have any questions for Mr. Hudson?"

The BLM attorney sprang to his feet. "I object, Your Honor. I wasn't given the opportunity to question Ms. Wilkes."

"You'll get your chance," the judge said. "Sit down."

Mr. Brown stood. "Did you have Ms. Wilkes's permission to land your helicopter on her property, Mr. Hudson?"

"I was doing what the BLM hired me to do. I don't know why she was shooting at me because I was saving her hayfield from being eaten."

"Yes or no, Mr. Hudson."

"No, but she was about to make me crash."

"Why didn't you just fly away if her skeet shooting disturbed you?"

"Because I had a job to do."

"And why did you buzz her farm first?"

"I was looking for those damned horses. Everybody knows she harbors them."

Mr. Brown feigned surprise. "Harbors them?"

"She's been asked to fence off that back part of her farm if she doesn't want us chasing the horses across there, but she refuses."

"So, you're saying that she knowingly lets these wild herds graze on her property?"

Hudson growled under his breath. "I have no clue what goes on in that crazy lady's head."

The judge looked at the BLM attorney. "You have any questions for your client?"

The young attorney shuffled his papers a bit, then stood. "Did you fear that Ms. Wilkes was going to harm you?"

"She had exploded targets in close proximity to my helicopter, then pointed that shotgun at me when I attempted to talk to her. I had no way of knowing if she'd shoot me or not. If she didn't want me on her property, then why did she lock up my chopper so I couldn't leave?" He sat back with a smug smile and crossed his arms over his chest.

"No further questions, Your Honor, but I'd like to recall Ms. Wilkes to the stand."

The judge nodded, and Hudson glared at Maggie when they traded places.

"Now, Ms. Wilkes. Is it true that you aimed your skeet launcher so the targets would fly close to Mr. Hudson's helicopter when you shot them?"

"I wasn't operating the launcher," she said. "My dog was. You'd have to ask her that question, but I didn't bring her to court with me."

The crowd tittered with suppressed laughter, and the judge permitted it since he couldn't hide his smile either.

The attorney scowled. "A prudent person would wait until the helicopter was gone from the area before shooting near it. Are you aware that you were putting Mr. Hudson's life in danger? That you could be charged with murder, or manslaughter at the very least, if you had struck his helicopter and he crashed?"

"I wasn't shooting at him," she said.

"No further questions, Your Honor."

"Mr. Brown. Do you want to ask anything else?"

Brown rose, his expression as smug as Hudson's had been. "Ms. Wilkes, do you shoot skeet competitively?"

"You know I do."

"Are you any good?"

"Five times regional champion. I've been shooting since I was big enough to hold a shotgun."

"What was your score in the last competition?"

"Fifty out of fifty. Perfect score."

"So, you were confident that you would hit the targets and not Mr. Hudson's helicopter."

"Absolutely."

"One more question. Why do you refuse to fence that back half of your thousand-acre farm?"

"I grow hay there for my livestock, but I leave the second cutting for the wild horses when their usual grazing areas go dormant for the winter."

"So, help me understand something. The BLM feels the wild herds are overgrazing federal lands, but they don't want them grazing instead on your private property?"

Maggie shook her head. "Doesn't make sense, does it?"

"No further questions," Brown said.

Tobie silently cheered. Brown didn't look all that intelligent, but he was a wily country lawyer.

The BLM attorney stood. "One more question?"

The judge nodded. "I'll allow it."

"If you don't mind the wild horses grazing on your property, why don't you just fence them in there?"

"Then they wouldn't be wild, would they?" Maggie's eyes turned cold, like blue lasers cutting through the young man. "The horses were there before the government let ranchers graze their cattle on that land. They want to run their cattle on federal land because it costs them a fraction of the expense of grazing large numbers on their own land, and they pocket the profits after they buy off certain politicians to keep those grazing rights."

"Is this the first time you've appeared in court because of the BLM practice of low-flying over your property?"

"No. I have a permanent injunction against them flying low over my fields. Mr. Hudson was in direct violation of that order."

"You tell 'em, Maggie."

The judge ignored this latest outburst from someone in the audience.

Brown turned to the judge. "Your Honor, I think it's clear that Mr. Hudson knew he was flying over Ms. Wilkes's property in spite of an injunction against it. His claim that he was trying to save her fields doesn't hold water after he accused her of 'harboring' the wild horses. Finally, he chose to trespass by landing his helicopter in her field rather than flying away when he incorrectly had the impression she was shooting at him. We are asking that Mr. Hudson pay a fine of one thousand dollars to the Maggie Wilkes Wild Horse Foundation for trespassing on her property, with the understanding that the county will pursue jail time for any future trespass."

"You have anything to add?" the judge asked the young attorney.

"Uh, we would like for Mr. Hudson's helicopter to be released from the sheriff's impound. He needs it to make a living."

The judge banged his gavel once. "This court orders that Mr. Hudson pay one thousand dollars to Ms. Wilkes's foundation. He can retrieve his helicopter after paying the towing fee and a hundred-dollar-a-day impound fee."

Hudson jumped up. "That's robbery, and this is a kangaroo court."

The judge banged his gavel again. "Two weeks in jail, Mr. Hudson, for contempt of court."

Hudson opened his mouth to say more, but the judge stopped him.

"I can make that thirty days if you have more you want to get off your chest."

Hudson's attorney grabbed his arm. "No, Your Honor."

"Bailiff, please take Mr. Hudson into custody so he can begin serving his sentence," the judge said.

The courtroom audience stood and applauded when the bailiff announced "All rise" for the judge to leave the bench.

As a deputy was handcuffing Hudson, his attorney lectured him. "We'll pay your fine and get your helicopter out of impoundment, but you better keep your mouth shut."

"I want to appeal this decision."

"Then you'll have to hire your own attorney. That judge is the governor's brother. You don't want to be messing with him."

"Wow. You were great up there," Tobie said. Until now, she had no idea of the extent of Maggie's fight to preserve the wild horses. "I don't understand why the government pours so much money into rounding up the herds rather than putting more funds toward a workable contraception program." She held the truck door open for Maggie, who climbed in. Tobie stowed the crutches in the back seat.

"They won't admit it, but their ultimate goal is to get rid of the wild horses altogether, or pen them up like they did to the Native Americans and turn the land over to cattle ranchers. Wealthy white men are greedy. The more money they amass, the more they want," Maggie said after Tobie rounded the truck and slid into the driver's seat.

"That's a pretty broad statement." Tobie said.

"I was speaking in general. We have plenty of good men around here. Ricky and Jake are two of them."

"I agree." Tobie eyed Maggie. "Is it bad that your performance in the courtroom turned me on? When you recited your skeet score, that was so hot."

Maggie smiled at her. "I thought I'd bust out laughing at your innocent act when you were explaining about Kate pushing the button to release the skeet targets. But then, it played right into his question about the targets intentionally aimed at his helicopter."

"That was so funny. I was afraid I was going to jail with Hudson for contempt of court because I almost fell onto the floor laughing," Tobie said as they pulled up next to Maggie's farmhouse.

When she helped Maggie out of the truck, Maggie grabbed Tobie's arm and twisted it behind her, then did the same with her other arm. "You're being held in contempt of my court, Ms. Mason, for almost making me laugh in court. March yourself inside to get your punishment."

"Yes, ma'am, Ms. Wilkes. I'm not sorry, so I deserve whatever you want to do to me."

They were inside and naked in minutes. Maggie pushed Tobie down on the bed. "Spread those legs for me, Mason."

Tobie obediently spread her legs, exposing her sex to Maggie's scrutiny.

"Do you like being ordered around?"

"I've never taken orders from anyone," she said. Truthfully, she wasn't sure. The feelings of excitement flooding her were new but not unpleasant.

Maggie thrust her hand between Tobie's legs and plunged inside. She pushed her legs up and used her hips to thrust her fingers into Tobie over and over.

The tingling began to build in her groin. "Oh my God, Maggie. Oh my God. I'm going to come."

"Not yet. I'm not done with you." She withdrew, ignoring Tobie's protest, and flipped her over. Then she lay against Tobie's back and entered her again from behind. She pushed inside with her thumb while using her fingers to stroke Tobie's engorged clit with each thrust of her hips.

Tobie had never been the submissive partner in bed, but this position and this woman were driving her higher and higher. Her orgasm hit like a tsunami, and she screamed Maggie's name. Still Maggie rode her until she climaxed again.

"No more," she begged. "I'm done."

Maggie withdrew and gently rolled her over, then cuddled against her.

Suddenly embarrassed by her wanton submission, Tobie couldn't meet her gaze.

Maggie stroked her cheek. "I didn't hurt you, did I? I kind of got carried away."

Tobie closed her eyes. "No. That was crazy good. Explosive." She stared at the ceiling. "I've just never been the submissive type in bed. I'm a little embarrassed at my behavior."

Maggie grabbed her chin to force her to meet her gaze. Her blue eyes were soft, and she continued to stroke Tobie's cheek. "Anything we do in the bedroom stays in the bedroom and between us. Always be honest with me if I suggest or do something you're not comfortable with."

"I'm not saying I didn't like it. I did. I'm just surprised at myself."

They were quiet for a while before Maggie spoke again. "Have you ever used a strap-on?"

Tobie felt her face heat. "Yeah, but I was always the one wearing it."

"Would you like to use one on me sometime?"

Tobie sucked in a breath. The thought of using a dildo on Maggie caused her hips to involuntarily buck.

Maggie smiled. "I'll take that as a yes."

"Yes." Her face heated again. "And maybe you could use one on me. It appears I might like that."

Maggie was about to answer when someone rapped loudly on the bedroom door. She groaned. "That better not be Judy again."

And it wasn't.

"You leave that woman alone, Maggie Wilkes. It's the middle of the afternoon."

They looked at each other. "Cindy," they chorused together.

"Get up. I brought supper. Y'all need to wait until nighttime to fuck around like normal people."

"I'm pretty hungry," Tobie said, laughing. Maggie shook her head, but they climbed out of bed and quickly dressed.

CHAPTER TWENTY

Tobie and Maggie fell into a euphoric routine over the next two weeks, their days spent milking goats, feeding livestock, and going to physical therapy sessions, while their nights were filled with stargazing and lovemaking. Heart's Run for Freedom fund was building, but so was the underlying tension of their undeclared future.

Then Tobie's month of vacation was more than over, and she had a lucrative contract to transport some cutting horses from Montana to Fort Worth before the winter snows began up north.

"Are you sure you'll be okay?" Tobie asked, pulling Maggie into a tight hug.

"I'll be fine. I'm in a walking boot now, and the physical therapist said I could spend a couple of hours a day without the boot as long as I don't decide to go jogging."

"You'll video-call with me?"

"Every night."

"I thought that insurance guy would come around this week since Dr. Weston sent him a final report that Heart was all healed, but I can't seem to get him on the phone."

"He'll have to wait until you get back, then. I don't think she'll be a priority for them until they have to turn in their quarterly report and account for expenses and losses."

"You're probably right." Tobie kissed Maggie long and deep. "Don't run off with any new haulers that might come through town while I'm gone."

"Well, you caught me there. I've got a new one coming in tonight, so you better hit the road."

"Yeah, right."

Maggie stole another quick kiss. "Please be careful. Don't get caught in any early Montana snowstorms."

"Weather reports show clear sailing." Tobie climbed into her truck and took one last, long look at the woman who cared so deeply about her friends and animals, the woman she realized she had come to care about just as deeply. The words were on the tip of her tongue, but she couldn't put voice to what her heart wanted to say—*I love you.*

❖

Maggie walked over to the door when she heard the big diesel truck pull up to the barn. She wasn't expecting Tobie for another three days, but her heart jumped for a split second when she saw the truck and fifth-wheel trailer until she recognized it wasn't Tobie's rig. The trailer was a livestock open rig with no defined stalls. She quickly strapped on her boot and hobbled outside.

A large man stepped down from the truck's cab and stretched his back before looking around.

"Can I help you with something?" she asked. Kate, always at her heel, growled.

The man took a clipboard from his truck and checked the paperwork attached to it. "Are you Tobie Mason?"

"No. She's out of town on business. I'm Maggie Wilkes. This is my farm." She had a bad feeling about this man and didn't offer her hand in greeting.

He scratched this beard and scanned the paddock before his gaze settled on Heart and Penny grazing in the adjacent pasture with the goats. "That the horse I'm supposed to pick up?"

"I'm sorry. You must be at the wrong farm."

He checked his paperwork again. "Nope. This is the address. I'm supposed to load one Thoroughbred mare, tattoo number X74826. A bay mare with one white sock."

"Was Ms. Mason expecting you today?"

"Lady, they don't tell me anything. They just put the paperwork in my hand and pay me to haul the horses on this list to Fort Worth for auction."

She hit speed dial on her phone. "Ricky, I need you at the farm, now." Then she hit a second number.

"Hey. I was going to call you tonight."

Maggie wasted no words. "A man's here trying to take Heart. Did you know about this?"

After a long silence Tobie finally answered. "I didn't think he'd be there until tomorrow. The insurance company called. I offered to buy Heart, but they insisted they want to see what they can get for her at auction."

"We've got forty thousand donated so far."

"They feel they might get more at auction. I told them that was ridiculous. They could possibly get that at a Keenland auction, but not at some stock sale in Texas. They insisted it was their protocol. I don't think the idiot I talked to knows anything about horses."

"I'm not giving her up," she told Tobie. "Gotta go. Ricky's here." She ended the call.

Ricky wheeled into the driveway, spraying gravel and sand, before hopping out of his sheriff's cruiser. "Aunt Maggie?"

"Lady, I don't want no trouble," the man said, eyeing Ricky. "I'm just here for a horse that belongs to the Five-Star Equine Insurance Company." He handed his paperwork to Ricky.

"This man wants to take Heart."

Ricky examined the paperwork, then looked up at Maggie. "I thought you guys were going to buy her."

"Tobie said the insurance idiots refused our offer. They think they can get more at auction."

Ricky shook his head. "I'm afraid his paperwork is in order. I can't stop him from taking her."

"God damn it. I should have set her free days ago instead of waiting for Tobie to get home."

The man took a halter and lead rope from his truck. "I'm sorry, ma'am. I've got my orders." He headed for the gate, and Kate circled him, growling. He kicked at her, but she was too quick for him to land a blow. "Call your dog off, lady. I don't want to hurt her."

"You kick my dog, and I'll shoot you where you stand."

The man kept walking to the pasture gate, not bothering to point out that she didn't have a gun with her.

"Kate, that'll do," Ricky called, issuing her a signal that she'd done all she could. Kate hesitated, then returned to Maggie's side.

Maggie hobbled after him, but her presence only brought Penny and Heart to the gate, looking for a scratch or a treat. The man stepped inside the gate, and, well trained, Heart lowered her head for him to slip on the halter.

"You don't even have a proper horse trailer," Maggie said, desperate to stop what was happening.

He led Heart from the pasture, ignoring Penny's raucous protest at being left behind. "I'm a careful driver, and we transport horses in these trailers all the time in Texas," he said. "She'll be fine."

"At least let me wrap her legs," Maggie pleaded.

He paused and looked at his watch.

"Ricky can make you a sandwich and some tea or coffee to take with you while I wrap her."

A smile spread across his face as he nodded. "That'd be right nice of you," he said. "A sandwich or two and coffee would be great. And maybe I could use your restroom? I've got a twelve-hour drive from here, and it'll save me a stop along the way."

"Sure. Come on inside, and I'll fix you up," Ricky said.

He started to hand Heart's lead over to Maggie, then stopped. "You're not going to set her loose, now are you?"

She shook her head. "I'm not a lawbreaker, mister. I'm just going to wrap her legs so the other horses you have in there don't clip her."

Three other horses peered out from between the metal bars on the top half of the transport. "That trailer holds six, and she's the last, so she won't be crowded," he said, taking a large thermos from his truck before following Ricky.

Maggie led Heart into the barn to crosstie her and wrap her legs for travel. "Don't you worry, sweetie. Tobie and I will be at that auction to be sure you make it back here."

Heart nuzzled Maggie's back when she bent over to wrap her front legs, as if to assure her that she'd be okay.

When she was done, she loaded Heart onto the trailer, pausing to examine the three horses already there. They appeared to be young quarter horses, all calm and in good condition. This was a favorable sign that she wasn't headed to a kill auction, but to a decent buyers' auction.

The truck driver and Ricky were walking back to the truck as Maggie was closing the trailer. The driver double-checked that she'd locked it securely, then offered his hand. "I'm real sorry about this, miss, but I'm just doing my job. I can promise you that she'll be in good hands as long as I have her."

She shook his hand. "Thank you. We'll be right behind you because we intend to buy her back."

He grinned. "I hope you do. Ricky showed me that video while the coffee was brewing. It sure tugs at your guts. The auction is in two days at the Fort Worth stockyards. It's a big place, though, so you'll probably have to do some asking around to find out exactly where."

"Thanks," Maggie said. "Safe travels."

❖

Maggie's phone buzzed instantly in her pocket as they waved the hauler down the driveway. She ignored it, knowing it was likely Tobie calling back. "Ricky, phone in and tell them you need a couple days off for a family emergency. Then go home and pack a bag. I'll go pack and make some more sandwiches. We're going to that auction to get Heart back."

"Are you crazy? Where's Tobie?"

"She's hauling a job, headed to the same destination but ahead of us. Go on, now. I can't drive all that distance with my left foot. I need your help."

"Yes, ma'am. Don't leave without me." He sprinted to his cruiser and tore out down the drive.

She hurried to pack a bag, filled a cooler with bottles of water and sweet tea, brewed another pot of coffee to fill two thermoses, and made a sack full of sandwiches from the pot roast she'd cooked the day before. Finally, just as Ricky was returning, she checked the website. They'd raised forty-five thousand dollars to buy Heart. It would just have to be enough.

They loaded everything into her truck, and Ricky drove while she made another call. "Cindy, I need you and Jake to look after the farm for a few days, starting with the milking tonight."

"What going on? Where are you going?"

"Ricky and I are on a rescue mission and are headed to Fort Worth. I'll explain later and call you when we're on the way back." Her phone buzzed with a second call, again from Tobie. "Gotta go. Tobie's on the other line."

"Wait. Maggie!"

She clicked over to the other call. "Tobie."

"I've been calling and calling. What's going on?"

"Sorry. Where are you?"

"I'm headed to Fort Worth."

"I know that. How close are you?"

"I've just passed Abilene."

"They have Heart and are taking her to an auction in Fort Worth, right where you're going."

"But the horses I'm hauling are going to a quarter horse auction."

"Well, there's apparently going to be at least one Thoroughbred in the middle of that auction."

"Weird, but they were probably able to do that because Five-Star Equine Insurance insures about ninety percent of the horses in the auction." She was quiet for a few seconds, then softened her voice. "Are you okay? I know how badly you wanted to save Heart."

"Damn right. And we aren't giving up. Ricky and I are headed to that auction. We'll meet you there."

"What? You can't drive with that boot on your foot. Tell me you haven't taken it off to drive twelve hours."

"Ricky's driving right now. I can take a turn a little on the interstate with my left foot to give him a break."

"I told you they wouldn't sell her to us."

"They can't control who bids on her in an auction. She's ours, and we're going to get her back."

"Maggie?"

"Yeah?"

"You are my Wonder Woman."

"I don't know about that, but I'm planning to do my best."

"I'll call you when I reach the auction yard to tell you where to find me. You guys be safe."

"You, too, love." The endearment slipped out before Maggie could stifle it, and she ignored Ricky's grin. "Shut up and drive," she grumbled.

Chapter Twenty-one

The truck was littered with sandwich wrappers and empty water bottles when they finally pulled onto the stockyard grounds. Tobie, who was parked in the sparse RV lot behind the stables, enveloped Maggie in a long hug.

"I've missed you this past week."

"Me, too, sweetie. Have you seen Heart?"

"I think you beat that hauler here. I've been watching for him, but I haven't spotted any rigs yet like you said he was driving."

"Is there a men's room nearby? My eyes are swimming," Ricky said.

"It's a bit of a walk. Use the bathroom in the camper," Tobie said.

Once they were alone, Tobie insisted that Maggie sit in one of the lawn chairs she'd set outside the camper. "Be honest. How's your leg?"

"I probably need to put it up for a while and use a little ice, but Ricky drove most of the way. I brought my crutches, though, because I figured I might have to walk more here than I need to do with just the boot."

"I'm glad to see you're not being too stubborn about it. You need to relax a while."

"We don't have time to rest," Maggie said. "We have to find where they're stabling Heart."

"How about we go locate some hot food, then look through the stables to see if she's arrived." Tobie opened the door to the camper.

"Hey, Ricky, we're going to get something to eat, then check the stables to see if Heart's here yet."

"Can you bring me something back? I want to update the website." He was sitting in Tobie's recliner with his iPad.

"Are you sure?"

"Yeah. You guys go ahead. I'm going to catch a nap after I finish this update."

"You're a good man, Ricky," Tobie said. And she meant it.

He looked tired, though he was grinning. "Thanks. I owe Aunt Maggie a lot. You take care of her, okay?"

"I'll try my best."

The stockyards was a sprawling campus with a thriving combination of cattle business, rodeo, retail stores, restaurants, and a Western theme park for entertainment. It was a little overwhelming, but they settled on a steakhouse for dinner, then walked the area where horses were stabled for the auction scheduled in two days. They had nearly given up finding Heart for the night when Maggie spotted the hauler who'd come to her farm.

"Hey, you're here. Where's our horse?"

"I'll be damned. I thought you were fooling when you said you were coming to buy her back." He removed his ball cap and rubbed his bald head. "I just unloaded, and they led her off in that direction," he said, pointing down one aisle.

The horses were assigned ten-foot by ten-foot temporary stalls separated by six-bar steel corral panels so prospective bidders had a clear view of each horse. They found Heart halfway down the hallway, in a clean stall with adequate bedding, a hay bag, and a water bucket. She nickered to them, and Tobie squeezed through the bars to unwrap her legs.

"Hey, lady. You aren't supposed to be in there." A young man with a badge identifying him as one of the staff frowned at her.

"Those are our leg wraps I put on her before she was shipped. She's been in them for over twelve hours, and they need to come off," Maggie said, using her crutch to block him from entering the stall and stopping Tobie.

"Are you the owners?" He checked the paperwork attached to Heart's stall and eyed Maggie suspiciously. "Says here that she belongs to an insurance company."

"We're the buyers, and we want her in top condition when we take her home."

He scoffed. "This is an auction, lady. She isn't yours until you outbid everyone else."

Tobie rolled the last leg wrap and exited the stall. "Chill, buddy. I'm done. And these are our leg wraps, so I'm taking them with me."

It was late, and Heart seemed settled, so they went back to Tobie's camper and woke Ricky to eat the steak they'd brought back for him. They decided that Maggie and Tobie would get a hotel room so Maggie could rest properly and ice her leg. The trailer's camper was tight quarters for three people, and the water tank was too small for three showers. Ricky elected to stay in the camper.

The closest hotel seemed a bit fancy for Tobie, but she could see the weariness on Maggie's face. She was exhausted, too, having arrived at the stockyards only a few hours before them and then spent that time filing her paperwork and unloading the horses she'd been paid to transport. It was a lucrative job, so she didn't mind handing over her credit card for the room. And although the hotel seemed fancy, they were surrounded by others dressed in jeans and Western boots and hats, and toting duffels rather than rolling suitcases.

Tobie smiled when Maggie sank back onto the plush bed and heaved a sigh of relief. "Tired, baby?"

"Exhausted. Take my clothes off for me. I'm too wiped out to do it."

"You don't have to ask me twice."

"Wait. Take yours off first."

"Okay." Tobie stripped down to her boxer briefs, then began to remove Maggie's clothes. "You want to sleep in your underwear?"

"Yes, because if you take those off, I'll be inclined to try something I'm too tired to follow through on."

Tobie laughed. "I hear you." She turned off the lights so only the bathroom light cast a soft beam of illumination into the room. Then she slid onto the bed, cuddling next to Maggie for a long moment before moving to her back and pulling Maggie close to her side, the way they had slept for weeks until the cast was removed. "I've got you, Wonder Woman. Just rest."

They began to drift into sleep within moments, Maggie's soft breath brushing Tobie's bare chest, and her heart beating against

Tobie's ribs. This is heaven, Tobie thought. But her experience had been that nothing lasts—not her parents, not her grandmother, and maybe not this bit of happiness she'd somehow stumbled upon.

❖

They brought Ricky a couple of breakfast burritos but found him at Heart's stall rather than in the trailer. He was ensconced in one of the folding lawn chairs from the camper, chatting with people who were strolling the stable complex with tablets or printed pages describing each horse's bloodlines and credentials. He was talking to an older man when they walked up.

"What the hell is a Thoroughbred from the racetrack doing at a quarter-horse sale?" the man asked.

"You'd think the insurance company was trying to slip one in on you, right? I guess they're trying to get high dollar for her from a buyer that only knows quarter horses." Ricky pretended to commiserate with the man.

"Still, that's a pretty good bloodline. I bet she'd produce a fantastic Appendix quarter."

"Appendix is too big for cutting," Ricky said. "These are mostly cutters in this auction."

"True, but I know a few guys that race quarter horses. This mare might make a good hunter for my daughter and could throw a pretty good racer with her bloodlines."

"How old's your daughter? You might have to hire someone to train the racetrack out of her. Besides, I don't know if she's worth the trouble to breed. Have you seen that scar under her belly? She might have too much scar tissue to produce milk." He took his foil-wrapped breakfast and coffee from Tobie and winked at them as he pointed to his right. "You want something fast? You should look at that colt at the end of the aisle. With an ass like that, I bet he'd go zero to sixty in two seconds."

The man bent to look under Heart's belly, and she reached between the bars to grab the bill of his hat. "Ha. A trickster, too, I see. Still, she's a beauty," he said, walking off toward the stall Ricky indicated.

Maggie shook her head. "What are you doing?"

"Nothing. Just helping folks realize Heart isn't the horse for them." He took a big bite of one burrito and hummed with pleasure.

"Those insurance guys won't be happy if they catch you," Maggie said.

"I'm not breaking any rules," he said. "Besides, I don't think they even have a representative here. They've just dropped her off and are hoping to get a fat check in the mail."

"It's not a bad idea," Tobie said, endorsing Ricky's ploy. "You sleep okay?"

"I slept great," he said. "That camper of yours is awesome."

"Thanks. I like it."

Maggie slipped into Heart's stall and put on her halter. "I'm going to walk her a bit to make sure she's not too stiff from traveling," she said.

"Hold on," Tobie said. "I'll walk with you."

Others were walking horses that had traveled, then stood in stalls all night, so no one seemed to notice them. Maggie was quiet while they made one round of the complex, then started on a second.

"So, when's your next haul?" Maggie asked, avoiding Tobie's eyes.

Tobie winced at the tentativeness in her question. "Actually, a guy approached me before you guys got here about transporting a couple of horses from this auction to his ranch in Spanish Fork, Utah."

Maggie frowned. "Where's that?"

"From your place, almost straight up 491 to 191. It's about eighteen hours from here, but only a third of that from ho…your ranch. I could drop Heart off on the way up." She'd caught herself before calling Maggie's farm "home." She hadn't offered, and, truthfully, they'd only known each other less than two months. Sure, their connection had been instant, even though Maggie had fought it, and Tobie had never had a relationship that lasted longer than a year. But something had seemed to click into place for Tobie in the weeks she'd spent at Maggie's. She hoped Maggie felt the same and that she wasn't just a fling to her.

❖

"Hey, Ms. Wilkes. Maggie Wilkes!" A young woman, trailed by a guy holding up his phone to video them, ran after them, waving her hand to flag them down.

They stopped and turned to eye her.

Breathless, she asked, "You're Maggie Wilkes, the wild horse advocate, aren't you?"

Suspicious, Maggie hesitated as Tobie took a protective step closer to her. "Who wants to know?"

The young woman held out her hand. "I'm Melanie Parker, online influencer. Maybe you've seen my podcast?"

Maggie shook her head. "Can't say that I have. I don't have time to listen to podcasts."

"I report on the horse industry and follow your website. I couldn't believe it when I saw the update that posted last night, saying you were here with Sarah's Heart. It's an amazing story, and if you have a few minutes, I'd like to interview you." She patted Heart's side. "Is this the famous horse?"

"Yes. It is, but I don't have time for interviews, Ms. Parker." Maggie tugged at Heart's lead to continue their walk.

"I have two million followers," Melanie said quickly.

Tobie put a hand on Maggie's arm to stop her. "Two million?"

"Yes. I saw that you guys are raising money to free Sarah's Heart, but the insurance company is refusing to sell her to you."

"Highest bidder will take her home, whether it's us or someone else," Tobie said.

"Please, if you could take just a few minutes, I'd love to link to her video on your website and the donation address."

Maggie frowned. She didn't know this woman and wasn't sure she wanted to trust her. Besides, she looked to be about sixteen years old.

"Aunt Maggie, wait." Ricky rounded the corner behind them. "Oh, good. They found you."

"Do you know her?" she asked Ricky.

"I've checked out her podcast. She's legit. You should talk to her."

"I don't know." She was still reluctant. "Are you sure she's not with the Bureau of Land Management, out to smear us for wanting to release Heart into a wild herd?"

"I'd be willing to sign a paper stating that I have no connection to the BLM." The young woman signaled to the guy following her, and he whipped out a notebook and began scribbling.

Ricky stepped in, holding up his phone. "Swear to that on camera, and that'll be good enough."

She turned to him and put her hand up, palm out. "Ready?"

"Yep."

"I'm swearing this statement on camera as a legally binding verbal agreement. Neither I, nor my podcast, has any connection nor has received any funding from the BLM or any ranchers seeking to rid federal lands of the wild horses."

"I don't know if that would stand up in court," Ricky said, "but I can tell you that it would go a long way with a jury if you had to sue her for misrepresentation."

"It can't hurt, Maggie," Tobie said.

After thinking a bit, she agreed. "Okay. We need all the help we can get, I guess."

Twenty minutes later, Maggie and Tobie had recounted how Heart got free and the injury she suffered during the storm that allowed her to be caught.

"Aren't you afraid the mare would get injured again if she runs with wild horses?" Melanie asked.

"How far did you travel to get here?" Maggie asked.

"I'm based out of Atlanta, Georgia," Melanie said.

"Have you walked around the stockyards at night?"

"Well, yes. Looking for material for my podcast."

"Alone?"

"No. I have Jason with me." She indicated the guy holding the camera.

"Still, you could have gotten mugged, or your plane could have crashed coming in from Georgia, or you could get sick from being around so many people. Tell me, have you had a measles vaccination? You know they have a lot of anti-vaxxers in this part of Texas and a measles outbreak."

"Yes. I know."

"Wouldn't you be safer if you stayed in your house and did all your interviews from your home studio?"

"Yes, but I wouldn't want to live like that."

"So, you'd rather be free to do as you please, even if it might occasionally put you in danger?"

"Good point. I get it."

Melanie turned to the phone camera her friend was holding up.

"To summarize, Sarah Carmichael's dying wish was for her horse to be able to spend her retirement running free. However, in the expectation of selling Sarah's Heart at a higher price, the Star Equine Insurance Company has turned down the offer Ms. Wilkes made to buy the horse. So, she and Ms. Mason are here at the Fort Worth Stockyard to try to purchase her. But this is an auction where the bidders have deep pockets, so they'll likely face some stiff competition. If you'd like to help Heart's Run for Freedom, clink on the link below, and also watch the video of the late Sarah Carmichael talking about her horse."

"That's awesome," Ricky said. "Hopefully, more people will donate. That man who was looking at her this morning came by again, but he brought his daughter. She seemed like a spoiled little rich girl but told her father she could probably show Heart in hunter competition. I'm afraid he's going to bid against us."

"How soon will you post this?" Tobie asked the influencer.

"I'm heading back to our hotel now and should have it up within the next two or three hours."

Maggie finally relaxed a bit. "Thank you, Ms. Parker. We can use all the help we can get."

"You're welcome." She started to go but turned back. "By the way, I've been a Wild Maggie fan for years. I'd love to actually see some of those wild herds one day."

"Sure." Maggie nodded. "If all goes to plan, and we're able to free Heart, I'll have Ricky video her release and send you the clip. Then when you're free, you can come out, and I'll show you the wild herds."

"That would be fantastic." She gestured for her friend to follow. "See you at the auction."

CHAPTER TWENTY-TWO

Tobie was quiet as they walked Heart back to her stall.

"Something bothering you?" Maggie asked. "Because we've already done the interview. It's too late to take it back."

"It's not that."

Ricky looked from one of them to the other, as if sensing they might need to be alone. "Uh, I'm going to head over to Billy Bob's bar and grab a beer, then maybe walk over to the rodeo arena and check it out. I'll catch up with you guys later." He hurried away.

Maggie stared at her. "So. What's bothering you?"

"That girl had a point. What if Heart's injured again? This mare isn't savvy like the wild horses, or she wouldn't have gotten hurt the first time." Tobie rubbed her face. "I'm not sure turning her loose is the best idea. What if I kept her as my riding horse? You have Penny."

"I told you. I have Penny only because I can't get her to stay out of the barn. Hell, out of the house. She refuses to be freed." She frowned at Tobie. "You've seen Heart call for Night. You've heard him calling for her. She wants to be free, Tobie."

"I don't know. Would it be so bad if that man bought her for his daughter? She'd live in a nice barn, on a nice ranch, and hunt seat competition is easy work."

"It consists of going round and round a show ring so the rider can show how well they can ride in an English saddle. How about we give you one circular route and let you drive it until you're too old? Then God knows who they might sell her to when the little rich girl gets tired of her and wants a different horse."

Tobie looked down and kicked at the dirt floor of the stable area. "Yeah. Maybe you're right. Still, I wouldn't mind keeping her to ride myself."

Maggie knew she should have stopped there, but she couldn't help herself. "If we're able to buy her tomorrow, we'll be using money donated to my wild horses foundation specifically for the release of Sarah's Heart to Night's group. As owner of that foundation, what happens to Heart will be my decision, and mine alone."

Tobie stiffened, her expression unreadable. "So, why am I here? Oh, right, to drop off some horses and maybe pick up another job. Speaking of that, I have a man I need to see." She turned and strode off.

"Tobie, wait." But Tobie continued to walk away. "Shit. This is why I don't do relationships," she told Heart as she put her back in the stall. "I'm going to go find Ricky."

❖

"You said what?" Ricky looked at her like she'd grown a second head.

"I told her that if we're able to buy Heart, whatever happens to Heart is nobody's decision but mine." Maggie downed her Crown and Coke, then signaled the bartender for another.

Ricky scowled at her. "Why didn't you just say 'you don't matter, even though we're sleeping together and the horse was supposed to be yours'?"

"The mare was never hers. She belonged to the man who bought her, and then to the insurance company."

Ricky dropped his chin to his chest. "That's not my point. You know, for a smart woman, you sure can be oblivious. I'm no expert on women, but even I'm not too stupid to see how that must have stung."

Maggie scowled. Why was she having to defend herself? "I didn't say anything that wasn't true."

"Dang, you're hardheaded. You could have said it a lot nicer. You practically slapped her in the face." He shook his head. "We don't even own the horse yet, and you've managed to pick a fight with the one woman who might be able to put up with your moodiness."

"Shit." He was right. In the short time they'd been sleeping together, Maggie couldn't imagine crawling into bed without Tobie's warm body next to hers. She slammed back the rest of her second drink. "Come on. Let's go find her."

Tobie stood in the doorway of the rowdy cowboy bar that the Uber driver had recommended. It was as large as a barn, with a long bar positioned on the opposite wall from a stage, where a band played a lively country tune. The huge dance floor was crowded with couples dressed in Western fashion. This was perfect. She needed a place to drown her thoughts and numb her hurt feelings with some strong alcohol.

She slid onto one of the few empty stools at the bar and held up her hand to get one of the bartenders' attention. "Whatever you have on draft and a couple shots of tequila," she said.

A fifty-something woman quickly poured a tall mug of beer from the tap and plopped down two shot glasses before reaching for a bottle of tequila and filling each. "Lime and salt?"

"Sure. Why not?" Tobie wasn't much of a drinker, so these two shots were probably her limit.

Most of the patrons were on the dance floor, and two other bartenders were taking care of the rest of the bar customers, so the woman lingered. "Doing some heavy thinking?"

Tobie downed a shot, then guzzled half her beer. "Trying not to think."

"One of those nights, huh?" She refilled the shot glass even though Tobie still had the second shot. "Man trouble?"

"Woman trouble." The minute she spoke the words, she wanted to suck them back. She was in a strange, heterosexual bar in Fort Worth, Texas. They might beat up gays for fun here.

But the woman only smiled, shook her head, and refilled the empty shot glass. "That's even worse." She turned away to fill drinks for a few other customers, then returned. "Men are simple, but women are a lot more complex. You have a fight with the missus?"

Tobie frowned, then sprinkled salt on her hand and licked it before downing the next shot and sucking on the lime wedge provided. She grimaced as the liquor burned its way into her chest. "She's stubborn and bossy and thinks she knows everything."

"Well, she must be a looker for you to put up with that."

"Damn straight. Got blue eyes that nearly hypnotize you." Tobie downed the third shot and finished her beer. She waved off the bartender's attempt to pour another shot, but thrust her empty mug at her. "No more tequila, but you can pour me another beer."

"Coming right up."

Tobie nursed her second beer while the band took a break and the bartender dealt with a rush of thirsty customers coming off the dance floor. What did she care if Maggie set Heart free? It was just a damned horse. And Maggie was a damned hard-headed woman. She closed her eyes, and visions of naked Maggie under her, then over her assaulted her. Hard muscles and soft skin. She shook her thoughts away. Recorded music was playing a few slow-dance tunes while the band rested. Damn, she wished the band would start up again so she could fill her head with loud music instead of Maggie.

The alcohol was already slowing and shuffling her thoughts into a confusing jumble, but it wasn't lifting her mood. Tobie nearly flinched when a warm hand landed on her shoulder. She looked up at the tall, handsome cowboy standing beside her.

"How about a dance?" he asked.

She heaved a sigh. "No thanks. I'm not in the mood for dancing."

"Aw, come on. One dance won't hurt you."

"No thanks. I just want to drink my beer in peace."

When he grabbed her right arm to pull her toward the dance floor, she stood and punched him with a hard left that made him stagger backward. The bartender was instantly in front of her, waving over the bar's bouncer.

"This one's had enough and needs to go home," the barkeep told the bouncer.

"She hit me," the cowboy shouted, holding his eye, which was already swelling.

"That's because you can't go around grabbing women. Now

pipe down, or everybody in the joint is going to know you're whining because a woman beat you up."

The bouncer, a huge man, steered the cowboy toward the exit. "You can go home or to another bar to drink, but you can't stay here," he said.

"Sorry about that," Tobie said to the bartender. "I don't usually hit people. He sort of took me by surprise."

"For your hand." The barkeep smiled and plopped a plastic baggie of crushed ice on the bar. "Did hitting him make you feel any better?"

Tobie accepted the ice for her hand and managed a few seconds of introspection. "He had a hard head, but, yeah. I do feel better." Her anger at Maggie was gone, though replaced with embarrassment at her immature exit—too embarrassed to face Maggie right now. An adult would have stayed and talked to Maggie about why she was feeling hurt and overlooked. Instead, she'd run off and left only a note reclaiming her trailer for her own use, and sending Maggie and Ricky to the hotel.

They walked the stables and everywhere around it. Maggie alternated between using crutches and hobbling along in her boot, until she couldn't go an inch farther. When they checked Tobie's camper-trailer for the third time, they found a note taped to the door.

Going to dinner with some prospective clients. Y'all take the hotel room tonight. There's two beds. I'll stay here with Heart.

"Boy, you really scared her off," Ricky said. "I guess the farm will be all mine next time the tractor runs over you and maybe succeeds in killing you."

"You're not funny. Let's go to the hotel. Looks like we're not welcome here."

"Correction. Looks like *you're* not welcome. Can you blame her?" He climbed into the driver's seat of her truck. "Damn, Aunt Maggie. I can't believe you've managed to screw this up. It's clear to everybody that y'all are a perfect match."

"Clear, huh? Says who?"

"Everybody. Even Mama. You're so intense and prickly sometimes, but Tobie is laid-back enough to put up with you."

"Me prickly? She's the one who took off and disappeared." She was angry that Tobie had blown them off, but she could deal with anger. It was a familiar emotion. It was the underlying fear that Tobie had decided she wasn't worth the trouble because she was… difficult sometimes. Blunt. Spoke without thinking. And maybe a little prickly at times. Damn it.

CHAPTER TWENTY-THREE

Four-year-old gelding, just getting started, but showing lots of potential his first time out. He's sired by..." The auctioneer droned on about the horse in the ring that was up for bidding, while Maggie scanned the bleachers for the tenth time from their seats on one of the upper rows.

"I thought she'd be here for sure," Ricky said.

She didn't reply but returned her gaze to the ring, then busied herself with the printed program provided to all bidders.

The bidding on the gelding rose, until the auctioneer slammed his hammer on the gavel and proclaimed him "SOLD."

"She's here," Ricky said at same time.

Tobie scrambled across the rows of seats. "Hey," she said as she sat on the other side of Ricky. "Did I get here in time? You wouldn't believe the business I've picked up around here."

Okay. Maggie felt the chill. Tobie's cheerfulness seemed forced, and she appeared to be avoiding Maggie's gaze. But they didn't have time to worry about that now.

"Next up," the auctioneer said, "we have something different for you. Coming into the ring is Sarah's Heart, a five-year-old Thoroughbred mare that earned eight hundred and fifty thousand during her racing career. Retired from racing, she's a maiden mare, but just imagine, boys, the speed she could breed into your quarter horses. Now, let's start the bidding at twenty thousand..."

Maggie waited until a woman across the way lifted her hand, and then the man who'd previously stopped by the stall tipped his hat to up her bid.

"How much money do we have?" Maggie asked.

Ricky consulted his tablet. "It was still at forty-six thousand, but I asked it to update, and I still have a spinning wheel. My internet connection in here is weak."

"I've got thirty thousand. Do I have thirty-two?"

The woman held her fingers up, indicating thirty-two thousand dollars.

"Better jump in here," Tobie said.

Maggie raised her hands, holding up three, five, and five fingers.

"I've got thirty-five thousand, five hundred," the auctioneer said.

The man glanced her way and smiled as he held up four fingers.

"Forty thousand, folks. I have forty thousand. Can I get forty-five?"

The woman who had been bidding shook her head. She was out.

"I've got forty thousand, folks. Going once, going twice…"

Maggie indicated a bid of forty-two thousand.

The auctioneer had barely accepted her bid when her competitor bid forty-five thousand.

"Forty-five thousand for Sarah's Heart. Going once, going twice…"

Ricky jumped to his feet. "Fifty-five thousand," he yelled.

"What are you doing? We don't have that much," Maggie said between clenched teeth, reaching up to pull him back down into his seat.

He grinned at them. "Yes, we do. We have more than that."

Tobie picked up his tablet and held it up for Maggie to see. Their updated total donations topped seventy thousand dollars.

"Did I hear fifty-five thousand?" the auctioneer asked.

Maggie nodded confirmation.

"How about sixty thousand? Sixty thousand for this Thoroughbred mare with Secretariat bloodlines?"

The man, who was the only other bidder, shook his head. Apparently, he would only go so deep in his pocket to spoil his daughter.

"We have a bid of fifty-five thousand. Fifty-five thousand.

Going, going..." He slammed his gavel down. "SOLD, for fifty-five thousand."

Ricky waved his ball cap in the air and whooped.

"You did it, you did it," Tobie said.

The impact of everything hit Maggie hard—her injury, arguing with the insurance guys, Heart's injury, their desperate efforts to raise money for her purchase, and finally their success in buying her freedom. She grabbed Tobie and hugged the breath out of her. "I'm sorry, I'm sorry. We'll do whatever you want with that mare."

They both knew there was no legal choice but to free Heart as the donors intended, but just the implication, the concession that Tobie's feelings mattered, was enough. Maybe she could get the hang of this relationship stuff after all.

CHAPTER TWENTY-FOUR

Tobie unloaded the last of the four horses, including Heart, from her trailer into Maggie's paddock for the night. Tomorrow, she'd reload the three quarter horses and transport them to Spanish Fork. It was near midnight, and winter's chill cut right through their light jackets. They were all very tired from the long drive. Ricky went inside to stoke up the house's woodstove, while Maggie and Tobie fed and watered the horses in the paddock.

Penny ambled over from the adjoining pasture to greet Heart and check out the new horses. But Heart's eyes were on the woods across the pasture. She raised her head high, nostrils flaring as she tested the wind. She let out a long, loud call, but there was no answering whinny. She paced the paddock fence but finally settled down with the others and nibbled at the fresh, fragrant hay Maggie had put out for them.

Ricky was already snoring on the couch, where he'd curled up with a pillow and blanket. Both Maggie and Tobie peeled off their clothes in a very unsexy, exhausted way to collapse onto Maggie's bed and grab a few hours of sleep.

When Maggie woke, she smiled immediately. Tobie lay sprawled on her stomach, one fist curled under her chin, tousled hair sticking up in multiple directions, and bare shoulders and arms peeking out from under the quilt. She was filled with a warmth she suddenly knew she didn't want to and couldn't give up. The sun's first rays were streaming through the sheer curtains, and she knew Tobie needed to get on the road early but had a lot to do before she could.

She brushed the hair back from Tobie's face and kissed her forehead. "Tobie, time to get up."

The hand curled under Tobie's chin shot out and pinned Maggie to the bed, pulling her close.

"Don't want to." Tobie mumbled but didn't open her eyes. "Want to stay here, with you."

Maggie chuckled and kissed her pouty lips this time. "And I'd like to stay in bed with you, but duty calls. I'm going to start some coffee while you take a shower to wake up." She slid out of bed as Tobie groaned and groped for her hand to pull her back. "Up, up. Those horses aren't going to drive themselves to Utah."

She went to the kitchen to find that Ricky had already started the coffee and was standing over a frying pan full of sizzling bacon. "That smells good," she said. "I'll scramble up some eggs to go with it."

"Tobie still asleep?"

"No. She's in the shower. She needs to get on the road pretty soon."

"What are you going to do with Heart?"

"Tobie'll only be gone overnight. I figured we'd deal with the mare when she gets back."

"Okay."

By the time Tobie appeared freshly showered and dressed, Maggie had rolled up a couple of breakfast burritos in foil and filled a thermos with coffee for Tobie to enjoy on the road. "Ricky's sweeping out the trailer for you and refilling the hay bags."

"He's very handy to have around."

They walked outside to load the horses, and Maggie pointed down the road to the left.

"He's getting married next month. I was thinking of deeding him the ten acres on the other side of that sorghum field as a wedding present. He and his fiancée can build a house and maybe a barn. He's marrying a farm girl, so she'll probably want her own chickens and space for a good-sized garden."

"That's a great idea, Maggie. He's lucky to have you for an aunt."

"I'm lucky to have him for a nephew."

Tobie put her breakfast in the cab of the truck and her bag of toiletries in the camper. Ricky had already loaded the horses, but Tobie double-checked the latches on the slant-load stalls before closing the back of the trailer.

Even though they'd ridden back in Tobie's truck together while Ricky drove Maggie's truck, they hadn't talked about their earlier disagreement. Ricky, who seemed to have an instinct for when he should disappear, was busying himself with something in the barn while they paused at the back of the trailer. Maggie knew they were both stalling but were at a loss about what to say and when.

Tobie suddenly enveloped her in a tight hug yet didn't say anything.

That old cold fear began to creep up Maggie's spine. "You are coming back, aren't you?" she asked, afraid the hug was some kind of silent good-bye.

"I want to come back. In fact, I'd like to keep coming back, Maggie Wilkes, as long as you can stand me." She held on so tight, Maggie couldn't pull back to see her face. "I'm not easy. I haven't had to think about anything except what I want and what I do for most of my life. But I want to try."

Maggie relaxed into the hug. "Do you think you can live with a bossy control freak who hasn't shared her life with anyone in twenty years?"

Tobie finally released her to take Maggie's hands in hers. "We'll never know if we don't at least try. I don't want to spend the rest of my life with regret and thinking 'what if.'"

"Me either. I know we've both been self-sufficient for a lot of years, and learning to be with somebody else could be challenging. We need to learn to let go of things once in a while." She looked up and searched Tobie's soft brown eyes. "But if you think about it, we're perfectly matched. You'll be on the road enough to give both of us the alone time we're used to. And maybe I could ride with you occasionally."

Tobie grinned. "Are you asking me to be your girlfriend?"

"I thought you already were," Maggie said, laughing.

"I guess I am." Tobie surged forward and kissed her like her last breath depended on it. She looked at Maggie when she drew back. "Because I've fallen in love with you."

Maggie scoffed. "There you go, getting all mushy on me." She eyed Tobie, then finally let her smile grow. "I guess I've kind of fallen for you, too."

Heart interrupted them with a loud, shrill neigh. She was looking out past Penny's pasture to the woods again. This time, Night answered and appeared at the forest's edge. He ran up and down the pasture's fence, calling to her.

"Those two really formed a bond while she was free," Tobie said. She squeezed Maggie's hand. "Sort of like us."

Maggie smiled. "Yes. It would seem so."

"I think it's time," she said.

Maggie studied her. "Are you sure? We said we'd wait until you came back to decide what to do."

Tobie held Maggie's hand to her chest. "We already know what we have to do. What we should do," she said. "Get her out of the paddock. I'll be right back."

Maggie slipped a halter and lead on Heart while Tobie went into the barn and returned with a bucket of farrier tools and Ricky in tow. Without a word, she went to work on the mare's feet, pulling her shoes and trimming her hooves to begin her shoeless life. Heart stood still for their removal but never took her eyes off the dark stallion calling to her. Ricky was filming the whole scene when Tobie put down the last hoof and straightened.

Night called again, and Heart answered.

Maggie turned to Ricky. "It's been a journey, and there are no guarantees in life, but we're here to make Sarah Carmichael's last wish for her horse come true."

"That's her stallion, Night, calling for her," Tobie said to Ricky's camera. "And this time, she's going to be able to answer." She removed Heart's halter, but the mare only stood there as if unsure what to do.

Night called again, and Maggie slapped the mare gently on the rump. "Go ahead. You're free now."

With that slap, Heart raced away, head and tail held high, to meet her stallion.

"We never tested to see if she was really pregnant," Tobie said.

"We'll know like I do with all the mares…when she starts showing," Maggie said.

They stared after the two horses long after they disappeared into the woods. Finally, Ricky broke the silence. "I'll send this video to Melanie, then get it up on our website, too," he said. "Right now, I'm going to see if I can take my fiancée to breakfast."

Maggie frowned. "You just ate breakfast."

He patted his trim stomach. "One burrito. I could eat again."

Tobie laughed, waving him on his way. "You better watch out, or you won't fit in your tuxedo for the wedding."

Maggie found herself in Tobie's arms again. "Are you sure about us?" she asked.

"I'm a little scared," Tobie said. "But if Sarah's Heart has the courage to run toward what will make her happy, risking it all to live her best life, then we're going to break free of my fears, too."

She walked Tobie to the cab of her truck. "I love you."

Tobie kissed her again. "And I love you. But I have one question."

"What's that?"

"When we go out to check on the wild herds and the trail cameras, what am I going to ride now that we let my saddle horse go?"

Maggie grinned. "My cousin has Penny's brother that he'd be willing to sell."

"A mule?"

"At least you'd be sure he'd always come back to the farm, because mules are too lazy to fend for themselves in the wild when they can have you feed them twice a day. Once you get one, you can't get rid of them."

Tobie laughed. "Sort of like me."

"Go on. You have horses to haul, and I have goats to milk."

One more kiss and exchanged warnings to be careful, and Maggie watched Tobie's rig make its way down the gravel drive to the highway, her mood light and heart ridiculously happy.

EPILOGUE

D o you see her?" Tobie edged closer, eager to take the binoculars from Maggie and look for herself.

"That's Night's group, and I think I've spotted her on the other side of the herd…unless they've picked up another bay mare as tall as Heart."

"Let me look." Tobie couldn't stand it any longer. She grabbed the binoculars from Maggie and scanned the horses herself. "That's her, all right. But I can only see her back. We need to circle around."

Maggie nudged Penny to skirt the pasture along the forest's edge, and Tobie followed on Nickel, Penny's half-brother. Tobie had been doubtful when Maggie urged her to buy him but found Nickel to be surprisingly smooth-gaited and, like Penny, absolutely committed to the luxury of barn life.

Night's group had grown accustomed to the two mules frequently tailing them and didn't move away as they rounded the field and drew closer. Tobie stood in her saddle and whistled long and low. Heart raised her head and moved toward them.

They both collectively sucked in a breath. Trailing at Heart's side was a new foal. Black like its sire and long-legged like its mother, the youngster kicked its heels and snorted at the mules, but came close when Heart walked up to accept a few carrots from Maggie.

"We probably shouldn't feed her treats like this," Tobie said. "I worry that she'll walk up to some other humans who might try to catch her."

But Night had other ideas. He called to his mare and flattened his ears at the newcomers. Heart obediently turned away and walked back to the herd while the foal raced circles around her.

"I don't think you need to worry. Night keeps a close eye on her. Besides, I don't think anyone but us can get this close to them, and that baby already runs faster than some of the yearlings."

"It's a colt," Tobie said, now that they'd had a closer look. Tobie looked the foal over. He was obviously thriving, so their fears that Heart wouldn't be able to nurse him were happily unfounded. "He looks healthy enough."

"With his mama's speed and his father's looks, he'll have his own family one day," Maggie said. "What should we name him?"

"How about Night Racer," Tobie said. "We can call him Racer."

"Yeah. I like it," Maggie said. She reached for Tobie's hand, as she often did, to relish their ever-growing connection. "Night Racer, sired by Night out of Sarah's Heart. Who knew that stormy-road pileup would be Heart's run to freedom and a new family?"

Tobie squeezed her hand. "I would have never guessed a trailer stuck in the mud would lead me to my heart's true love."

"Oh, God. Don't be mushy," Maggie said, pulling a long face as they turned their mules back toward the farm.

"You love it." Tobie loved to tease her very practical partner. "You know you do. Just wait until we get back to the farm. I'll show you mushy."

Maggie laughed and kneed Penny into a canter. "You'll have to catch me first."

Tobie hooted and urged Nickel to catch up to them. "I think I already did that."

About the Author

D. Jackson Leigh grew up barefoot and happy, swimming in farm ponds and riding rude ponies in rural Georgia. She has retired from her career as a journalist but continues her real passion—writing sultry lesbian romances laced with her trademark Southern humor and affection for dogs and horses.

She has published 19 novels and one collection of short stories with Bold Strokes Books, winning five Golden Crown Literary Society awards in paranormal, romance, and fantasy categories. She was also a finalist in the romance category of the 2014 Lambda Literary Awards.

You can friend her at facebook.com/d.jackson.leigh.

Books Available From Bold Strokes Books

The Art of Love by Ali Vali. When Mimi and Bianca both set their sights on Jolly, sparks fly, loyalties are tested, and hearts collide as they navigate the unpredictable nature of their hearts. (978-1-63679-719-9)

Chasing Her Scent by MJ Williamz. When Sheridan Rousseau walks into Lisette Mouton's charming little bookstore in Quebec City, she unknowingly holds the key to a mysterious box hidden in a secret room. (978-1-63679-900-1)

Heart's Run by D. Jackson Leigh. Hoping to recover an escaped racing mare, stock transporter Tobie Mason locks horns with local wild horse advocate Maggie Wilkes. (978-1-63679-825-7)

Scandalous by Kris Bryant. When a Hollywood actress trades places with her twin sister, everyone's in an uproar about getting duped, but Lindsay's more concerned about finding out which twin she made out with. (978-1-63679-874-5)

The Secrets of Rhydian Hill by Ronica Black. A doctor in need of a new start. A woman running from a killer. A love story that could end in tragedy. (978-1-63679-880-6)

Feeling Lucky by Krystina Rivers. What happens when, despite suddenly having enough money to buy almost anything, Lucy and Tanner start to discover that maybe all they need is each other? (978-1-63679-876-9)

Iceberg by Gun Brooke. When Lady Arabella hires Zandra, she never expects to find love, especially not as a disaster looms on the horizon. (978-1-63679-908-7)

It Happened One Semester by Aurora Rey. After a Pride night hookup, can eager new Assistant Professor Hudson Greene and Dean of Advising Callie Shaw overcome the odds and ace falling in love? (978-1-63679-814-1)

It's Kind of a Bad Idea by Sarah G. Levine. What happens when an emotionally unavailable serial dater meets the one woman she can't help but fall for—who happens to be the one woman who told her not to? (978-1-63679-920-9)

Thankful for You by Tagan Shepard. Everyone deserves to find their person. Maybe Karen has finally found hers? (978-1-63679-884-4)

What Happens On Location by Nan Campbell. How can Helen produce a successful movie when its director is the woman responsible for the demise of her marriage? (978-1-63679-904-9)

When Love Comes Around by Radclyffe and Ronica Black. Can Maya Sanchez and Nolan Wright trust each other enough to build something real, or will the past tear them apart? (978-1-63679-930-8)

Anywhere with You by Margo Glynn. On a road trip through the Great American Southwest, two friends discover nature, hope, and each other. (978-1-63679-907-0)

Burning Bridges by Lesley Davis. Can Clancy and Jude crack the case of eight missing women—and the secrets of their own hearts? (978-1-63679-872-1)

Dreams Entangled by Sophia Kell Hagin. Amid self-doubt, secrets, a pandemic, fear of attack and attempted murder, Pirin and Gracie's attraction turns to love, and their lives will never be the same. (978-1-63679-892-9)

Echoes of Love by Catherine Lane. As Hazel's and Jo's paths intertwine, they're swept up in a whirlwind of long-buried secrets, sizzling chemistry, and memories that won't be denied. (978-1-63679-835-6)

The Fame Game by Ronica Black. Wild child Hollywood actress Luna Kirkman begins dating Hollywood's leading man, only to fall for his straitlaced sister instead. (978-1-63679-858-5)

Moonlight Obsession by Sheri Lewis Wohl. All it takes to stop a clever killer is moonlight, love, and a silver bullet. (978-1-63679-831-8)

My Boyfriend's Wife by Joy Argento. Amid betrayal and heartbreak, can two women discover a love that could heal their pasts and rewrite their futures? (978-1-63679-866-0)

Tapout by Nicole Disney. A struggling MMA fighter finds her edge in an underground ring, but as she falls for the magnetic and ambitious promoter behind the matches, their dangerous world threatens to destroy everything they've fought to rebuild. (978-1-63679-924-7)

An Extraordinary Passion by Kit Meredith. An autistic podcaster must decide whether to take a chance on her polyamorous guest and indulge their shared passion, despite her history. (978-1-63679-679-6)

Heart's Appraisal by Jo Hemmingwood. Andy and Hazel can't deny their attraction, but they'll never agree on the place they call home. (978-1-63679-856-1)

That's Amore by Georgia Beers. The romantic city of Rome should inspire Lily's passion for writing, if she can look away from Marina Troiani, her witty, smart, and unassumingly beautiful Italian tour guide. (978-1-63679-841-7)

Through Sky and Stars by Tessa Croft. Can Val and Nicole's love cross space and time to change the fate of humanity? (978-1-63679-862-2)